FOLLOW THE ELEPHANT

OTHER BOOKS BY
BERYL YOUNG

Wishing Star Summer
(Raincoast Books, 2001)

Charlie: A Home Child's Life in Canada
(Key Porter Books, 2009)

follow the
ELEPHANT

To Hope

BERYL YOUNG

Happy writing

Beryl Young

RONSDALE PRESS

FOLLOW THE ELEPHANT
Copyright © 2010 Beryl Young

RONSDALE PRESS
3350 West 21st Avenue, Vancouver, B.C., Canada V6S 1G7
www.ronsdalepress.com

Typesetting: Julie Cochrane, in Minion 12 pt on 16
Cover Design: Julie Cochrane
Paper: Ancient Forest Friendly "Silva" (FSC) — 100% post-consumer waste,
    totally chlorine-free and acid-free

Ronsdale Press wishes to thank the following for their support of its publishing program: the Canada Council for the Arts, the Government of Canada through the Book Publishing Industry Development Program (BPIDP), the British Columbia Arts Council, and the Province of British Columbia through the British Columbia Book Publishing Tax Credit program.

Library and Archives Canada Cataloguing in Publication

Young, Beryl, 1934–
    Follow the elephant / Beryl Young.

ISBN 978-1-55380-098-9

    I. India — Juvenile fiction. 2. Grandmothers — Juvenile fiction.
3. Grandparent and child — Juvenile fiction. 4. Pen pals — Juvenile
fiction. I. Title.

PS8597.O575F64 2010   jC813'.6   C2009-906342-5

At Ronsdale Press we are committed to protecting the environment. To this end we are working with Canopy (formerly Markets Initiative) and printers to phase out our use of paper produced from ancient forests. This book is one step towards that goal.

Printed in Canada by Marquis Printing, Quebec

To splendid travelling companions:
my son Jeremy and my grandson Cameron

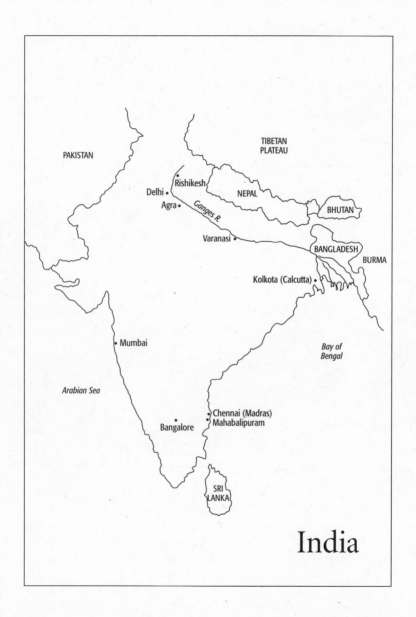

India

You Want Me To Go *Where*?

"GET OUT OF MY ROOM!"

His mother glared at him. "Then take your face out of that computer, Ben, and be downstairs in two minutes!" She turned and went back down the stairs.

Ben banged the table with his fist, making his computer mouse jump. Why did his mother make him so mad? He knew it wasn't her fault that his dad had died. But it wasn't his either.

These days his mother moped around the house and never got dressed up, even though she'd started back to work. She kept serving the same old boring stuff for meals as though nothing mattered now that they weren't a real family. He was mad at that nine-year-old brat Lauren too. She was back telling dumb knock-knock jokes as though things could still be funny, even with their father dead.

Everything was different now. There was no Dad to crack jokes at the dinner table, no Dad to go with on bike rides out to the university. No Dad to take him to hockey games. He remembered how excited his dad would get when the Canucks scored a goal. He'd punch Ben on the arm and say, "How's that for a great shot, Beno!"

Just about the only thing that had kept his father from being perfect was that he smoked. Most of Ben's friends thought smoking was definitely lame. Life skills class drummed that into you in grade three. When his father coughed it sounded like the old dog next door barfing up his dinner. His father's lungs were probably as disgustingly black as the pictures the teacher showed in class. Ben used to hide the cigarette packages and beg his father not to smoke.

More than once his dad would announce, "Well, I've finally done it. This is the last of these little killers you'll see in my hand."

Of course they all believed him, and it worked for a while — then one day Ben would catch his father in the garage again sneaking a smoke. How could a kid look up to a father who did that?

One day his dad had said, "I started smoking when I was young, Ben, and I thought nothing could hurt me. Now it's too hard for me to quit." He'd ruffled Ben's hair. "Don't you make the same mistake." That same week his dad had cut down. But it was too late.

Then, after his father had died, the stupid hospice counsellors kept asking Ben if he'd like to talk. Ben had nothing to say. He'd been cheated out of having a dad around. End of story.

What was the point of it all if your father died when he was still in his forties? What was the point of anything? That was why Ben liked computer games. You never had to think about sad things when you were fighting an alien on *Battlefront*. Computer games were easy. You knew what you had to do.

Of course his mother spazzed because he spent so much time on the computer. But why not play on the computer? It was way more interesting than school.

School. Well, he'd got himself into a bit of trouble there too. His friend Mac had talked him into skipping the first time. It had been simple just to disappear after lunch and fun to hang out at the mall gawking at all the new computer stuff. He'd do it again if he got a chance.

As far as Ben could tell, things would be easier if his mum and dad had divorced. Kids with divorced parents still had their dads to do things with. Like Jimmy, whose dad had taken him salmon fishing up at Campbell River last summer. There was a picture of Jimmy with his father on his bedroom wall, both of them holding up twenty-pounders.

Ben came into the living room where his mother and his

grandmother were sitting together on the sofa. Gran was his dad's mother, and since his father died she was always at the house. Ben thumped himself down in a chair, crossed his arms and jammed his fists into his armpits.

Gran offered him some licorice, but he shook his head. Sweet things were his grandmother's weakness. She wasn't fat, but she was always moaning about gaining weight and needing more exercise, yet somehow she always had candy to pass around.

"We're worried about you, Ben," said his mother, leaning forward with her elbows on her knees. Her blue eyes locked into his the way only a mother's eyes could.

Ben looked away. "Don't waste your time."

His mother pulled out the scrunchie in her ponytail, ran her fingers through her streaky brown hair and twisted it up again. "Ben, you've changed since your father died. You're rude and bad-tempered all the time. You pick fights with Lauren. You bury yourself in violent games and heaven knows what else on that computer. I never see you reading a book. Then last week you skipped school."

"So? Lauren bugs me and I told you the truth when I said I'd never skipped before. Besides, computer games aren't violent. *Battlefront* and games like that are good for improving your reaction time." Ben scowled across the room. "Why can't you just butt out of my life?"

"Sorry, we can't do that," his mother said. She looked as though she might start to cry, but then got herself together.

"I guess I haven't been the greatest mother lately. In the months since Dad died, I've been a bit lost myself."

Ben suddenly wanted to go over and give her a hug, but his shoes were Crazy-glued to the floor and he didn't move.

Gran interrupted. "Ben, I've come up with an idea, and I need you to listen. Don't say anything until I've finished."

What was Gran's brilliant idea now? Private school? A foster family? He was too young to be sent into the army.

Gran went on. "A long time ago when I was in grade school, my teacher gave me the address of a girl who lived in India. Her name was Shanti Mukherjee and she became my pen pal."

"What's a pen pal?"

"It's someone you write back and forth to. We actually wrote letters in those days!" Gran laughed. "Shanti was my age and she went to an Indian girls' school where she'd learned English."

"What does this have to do with me?" Ben asked.

Gran took a deep breath. "I was an only child and I shared everything with Shanti. When I was sixteen my mother died, and Shanti wrote letters that made me feel she understood how sad I was." Gran brushed her grey hair off her high forehead.

"So?" said Ben, swinging his leg over the chair. "You think I need a pen pal?"

His grandmother took a small black-and-white photograph from her wallet and handed it to Ben. It was a picture of a dark-skinned girl in a school uniform, her hair in thick braids. On the back was written, *Shanti Mukherjee, aged 13.*

My age, thought Ben. "Why are you telling me all this?" He put the photo down on the coffee table.

His mother looked at him sharply. "Please let your grandmother finish!"

"Shanti and I hoped we'd meet one day, but then, after years of writing, we had a disagreement and I never heard from her again."

Ben picked at his fingernail. "Can I go now?"

Gran handed Ben an airline ticket. She was smiling. "I want you to come to India with me to find her."

Yikes. Ben stared at the ticket with his name on it.

> Benjamin Leeson
> Air India Flight 860
> Vancouver, Canada, to Delhi, India
> January 2 to 19

"Oh, man." He couldn't think of anything else to say.

Lauren came bouncing into the room. "Does he know? Did you tell him?"

"Yes, and for once he's speechless," said their mother.

"Lauren knew about this?" asked Ben.

His sister flashed her lopsided grin at him. "Yeah, Mum's worried you're turning into a computer geek."

Ben leaned over and gave Lauren a shove. He glanced again at the ticket. "I could go seventeen days without a computer. And I could definitely use a break from a smart-mouthed sister."

"Easy, easy," said his mother.

Ben got up from the chair. "That is, if I wanted to. But there's no way I'm going to India." He headed for the stairs.

"Come back here, Ben," said his mother.

He leaned in the doorway, banging the heel of his runner against the frame.

"Stop that, Ben," his mother said.

"I know you weren't expecting this," Gran said. "I want you to think about it."

He gave one more kick and stopped. "You're okay about me missing school?" He looked at his mother.

"I checked with the school counsellor. You'll have to write a report on India when you get back," she said.

Considering he knew zip about India, that would be a challenge. All he knew was that India was a hot country halfway around the world. Sure, he'd planned to travel in a few years, maybe even go to India or Thailand, but definitely not with an old lady.

He shook his head. "No way."

"It's a wonderful chance to see a new country," said his grandmother.

"Tell someone who cares," said Ben.

"Benjamin!" his mother said.

"Don't be so mean to Gran," Lauren said. She flung her arms around her grandmother's neck.

"The tickets have already been paid for, Ben," Gran said,

"and as you can see we're booked to fly right after the holidays."

"You and Mum are so nervy. I can't believe you did this without asking me!" Ben felt like smashing a hole in the door.

Gran carried right on talking. "You'll need a passport and a visa for India. We'll get onto that right away. I'll take you for a passport photo next week."

"What bugs me most is that you told Lauren before you told me!"

Ignoring him, Gran said, "One more thing."

"What?"

"You and I have an appointment at the immunization clinic for shots. Typhoid. Hepatitis. Meningitis. Cholera. Starting Monday."

Ben felt as though he'd been put on a rollercoaster and things were going too fast. "It doesn't seem to matter what I think anyway," he snapped on the way to his room.

The next morning, Ben found his mother having coffee at the kitchen table. The chair where his dad used to sit across from her was empty. Ben slid into it and examined the big splats of rain hitting the window, then turned to his mother. "Why do you want to get rid of me anyway?"

"What makes you think that?"

"Because you're always mad at me. You yell at me all the time. 'Take out the garbage. Stop bugging Lauren. Get off the computer.'"

"Just how long *is* it since you've emptied the dishwasher, Ben?" His mother drained her coffee cup. "Think about it. I'm at the office all day and then have to do everything in the house, too."

Ben raised his eyes to the ceiling. Here we go, he thought. Mum was getting herself worked up.

"You've always got your nose buried in your computer or that PlayStation thing. I do all the laundry, the shopping and the cooking. You never offer to help out."

Ben could see tears welling up in her eyes. He hated that.

"I guess you want a medal?" Ben said.

His mother covered her face with both hands. He'd gone too far. "Mum, sorry. I didn't mean it to come out like that." He reached over and tapped her shoulder.

His mother's voice was muffled. "Why are you so angry all the time?"

Ben took a minute to answer. "Maybe because I miss Dad."

His mother put her hands down. Her face was smeared with tears. "Don't you think I do? And Gran? Lauren too?" Her voice cracked. "We're all lonely for him. We all miss the special things we did with him."

Ben had to turn away so he didn't have to watch more tears. His mother tried to steady her voice. "You know I don't want to get rid of you, Ben. I thought it would be good for you to have an exciting holiday."

"I don't want to go to India with Gran," Ben said. "She's too old."

"Gran's sixty-eight, Ben, and except for a bit of high blood pressure, which is totally under control, she's strong and healthy."

"I can see it all. I'm gonna end up being a granny-sitter."

"You've been asking for more responsibility, Ben. This is your chance to take care of your grandmother *and* yourself." His mother got up and stood behind his chair, wrapping her arms around his chest, pulling him close, like the old days.

Ben spread his fingers on his mother's warm arms. "Gran can be strict."

"Remember you used to say that about Dad, too."

Ben could barely remember that his dad had been strict. He was forgetting already. He leaned back against his mother.

"I'd have to get all those shots."

"Hey, a tough guy like you can't be scared of a few shots." Mum rested her chin on Ben's dark hair.

"Course I'm not."

"Good. I don't want my boy coming back from India with hepatitis. You don't look good in orange!"

He turned around and made a funny face at her. It felt good to laugh with his mum. They hadn't done that much lately.

All of a sudden his mother seemed like her old self. "Why not just go for it, Ben?"

Ben wasn't certain how it happened, but in a few days he'd had a photograph taken and had applied for his passport and visa. It sounded cool, having a passport. Teenage world traveller. Not bad.

He and Mum had spent an entire afternoon shopping. He bought cotton shirts, new runners and a large backpack with a lock and a small thermometer attached to the zipper.

"No way I'm wearing shorts," Ben had told his mother. "Jeans are fine." What kind of a guy would expose his skinny white legs all over India?

Then there were all the shots at the public health office. The first day he had three, one needle after another. Once you got used to them they weren't that bad. He and Gran filled their prescriptions for malaria pills and were told to take one after breakfast every day of the trip. The guys at school had been impressed when he told them about malaria pills.

This was the first Christmas without his father. On Christmas morning Mum gave Ben a digital camera with a zoom lens, saying she wanted to make sure she and Lauren got a look at India too. Lauren gave him a red baseball cap with CANADA written across it and a maple leaf on the visor. Gran gave Ben a cool pocket knife and told him, "They say never to eat Indian fruit if you can't cook it or peel it."

The family gave Gran a guidebook, *India: Land of Adventure*, with a photograph of a trumpeting elephant on the cover. Ben had seen the photograph when he'd helped Mum wrap presents. The huge beast was marching through the jungle, its trunk raised in the air, its ears flared like sails. The elephant was terrifying and fascinating at the same time.

"Look at this," Gran said. "On the first page it says, 'A

traveller goes to India seeking adventure. What he finds is himself.'"

"Find myself? I'm not lost," Ben said.

"Maybe you are," Mum said, looking right at him.

At Christmas dinner, Gran and Mum told Uncle Bob and Aunt Sheila and their eight-year-old son Marvin about the trip.

"Crazy idea!" Uncle Bob said. "India's 14,000 kilometres away."

Aunt Sheila asked why Gran and Shanti had stopped writing to each other.

Polishing off her second helping of plum pudding, Gran put down her fork, patted her stomach and sat back in her chair. "Shanti and I were both in our early twenties and she wrote that her parents had picked out the man she was to marry. I wrote back and said I would never let my parents pick out a husband for me."

"I'm going to pick out *my* own husband, that's for sure," said Lauren.

"As if," Ben said, sharing a look with Marvin.

"Then what happened?" asked Aunt Sheila.

"When I didn't hear back from Shanti in several months I realized I'd hurt her feelings. I knew I shouldn't have challenged a strong Indian tradition, and I wrote again, apologizing." Gran took a long breath. "But I never heard back from her. I thought either she was too angry to write or her new husband wouldn't let her."

Gran shook her head. "I didn't know what to do. So I did nothing." She was quiet. "I lost a dear friend and I want to try to make it right with her before I die."

"You don't have a clue where Shanti is now?" Uncle Bob said.

"I don't, and almost fifty years have gone by," Gran said. "But I feel she's still alive, somewhere in India. Of course, even if Ben and I do find her, she might refuse to see me."

Oh, wouldn't that be great, Ben thought. We go all the way to India, find this old lady and she slams the door in our faces.

"Gran, did you ever try to find her?" Lauren asked.

"Yes, I had the name of her school. It was the Calcutta Senior Girls' School. I wrote there ten years ago, but I never heard back. I think it no longer exists. The Indian consulate here in Vancouver told me I'd have better luck tracing her through marriage records at the central registry office in Delhi. Our plane lands in Delhi and I want to go there as soon as we arrive."

Ben watched his grandmother. Her broad face and strong jaw reminded him of his father. He'd inherited his own brown eyes from them. Ben had always loved Gran; he just wasn't sure about going on this crazy trip with her.

Marvin burst out, "India is full of snakes and elephants!"

"I hadn't thought about that," Gran said. "I am terrified of snakes!"

"Seeing a real elephant would be awesome," Ben said.

"This is a crazy quest you've set yourselves," Uncle Bob

said. "Seems to me it's about as impossible as finding the hair of a camel in the desert." Aunt Sheila was the only one who laughed with him.

"Well, here's fifty dollars for the trip, Ben," Uncle Bob said, handing a bill to Ben.

"Thanks," Ben said. He put it in his new wallet and closed the Velcro strap.

"Watch out for yourselves, you two," Uncle Bob said. "India's not an easy country. Only drink purified water. Take your malaria pills."

"We'll be fine." Gran nodded across the table to Ben.

"Whatever," Ben said on his way out of the room.

Day One

HIS MOTHER AND LAUREN had come to the Vancouver airport to say goodbye. Gran appeared dressed for the trip in a brown skirt the colour of a soldier's uniform. It came almost to her ankles, and with it she wore a matching brown hat with a wide brim and holes in the sides. She looked as though she were going on a safari.

"Why does the hat have holes?" Ben asked.

"To let my head breathe," Gran said. "It's a Tilley hat."

A black pouch was fastened around her waist and bulged over her stomach. She put both hands on it and patted. "Everything I need is right next to me in my fanny pack."

More like a funny pack — it was ridiculous. He was on a 747 on his way to India with a weird-looking old woman.

Ahead of them they had a nine-hour flight to London with a short stopover in the airport, then another nine hours to Delhi. It was going to be long and boring, but Ben had prepared for it. As soon as they'd settled in their plane seats, he turned on his PlayStation and put in earphones.

"What's that?" Gran asked.

"My PSP." Ben kept his eyes on the screen.

"What?"

He took out one earphone. "It's a PlayStation Portable. I can listen to music and play games on it."

"What games?"

"*Star Wars. Battlefront. Dungeon Explorer.* Games like that."

"I can't believe you brought the thing with you," Gran exhaled a long breath. "I hope you're not going to keep those plugs in your ears all over India."

"That's the idea."

"Not a good one," Gran said. "I'd hoped you and I would have a chance to talk on this trip."

"Talk about what?"

"About you." Gran leaned toward him. "You're still so angry about your father dying."

Ben put the earphone back in. "You could say that."

"Listen to me, Ben. We're together for more than two weeks. I'd like to help you talk about your feelings," Gran said. "Please take out those plugs when I'm talking to you!"

"There's nothing to talk about, Gran. You can help me by leaving me alone."

Gran glared at him, then picked up her book on India.

Ben flipped through the list of the movies available on the plane but he'd seen most of them. He stared out the small window. At 37,000 feet, the sky was a cold, unbroken blue. He played a few games on his PlayStation. Gran dozed and woke with a start as the attendant brought them each a meal.

When the pilot announced they were landing at London's Gatwick airport, he suggested passengers change their watches. It was now the morning of the next day. On-going passengers weren't allowed to leave the plane during the stopover, and all Ben could do was look out the window at the large planes on the tarmac. He couldn't even say he'd set a foot in England.

For the last eight hours of the journey, Ben decided to watch some movies he'd already seen. When the attendant put down breakfast trays with scrambled eggs and toast, Ben realized he'd fallen asleep.

As the plane descended, Ben and Gran had their first view of India. Below them, Delhi stretched like an enormous jigsaw puzzle across the landscape. Thousands of tin roofs, interspersed with parks and large buildings, went on as far as they could see.

Passengers cheered when the plane made a smooth landing, and they stepped out onto a metal stairway leading down to the tarmac. The air glittered with heat, burning Ben's eyes as he followed Gran and the other passengers toward the nearest building.

The long line for customs and immigration moved slowly. Passengers were tired and the room smelled worse than the boys' locker room at school. The serious uniformed immigration officer stared hard at Ben's passport photograph, then up at Ben and across to his grandmother. After a pause, he stamped their visas and passports.

Next, there was lineup at the money exchange. Ben studied the tariff, trying to figure out Indian money. Forty rupees to a dollar. For his fifty dollars he was given two thousand rupees in small red bills. It made quite a pile. Gran handed over five hundred dollars, and a high stack of bills and some silver coins came back across the counter. She stuffed the bundle inside her fanny pack and did up the zipper. Ben tucked his wallet into his pocket, and they headed for the terminal door.

In the brilliant sun of the Delhi afternoon, a noisy crush of men rushed toward the exiting passengers. Calling and gesticulating, the men tried to attract people to their taxis that were lined up in rows on either side of the terminal.

"This is scary. Hold onto your pack, Ben," Gran said.

Drivers pushed and shoved at each other to be the first to secure passengers. At one side, a tall, almost bald man smiled politely at Ben. Ben nudged Gran. "That man looks okay. Ask him."

Gran nodded and went up to the man, asking, "Could you please take us to the Hotel Mahal?"

"My honour, memsahib," the man said, taking Gran's backpack. He led them down the side, past rows of more men selling trays of cigarettes and gum, and stopped at a small grey taxi.

"My name is Madhu," the man said, bowing with his hands in a prayer position at his chest. "*Namaste.*" A smaller man who had been leaning against the taxi jumped up. "This is my friend Padam."

Padam greeted them with the same clasped hands, gave a high-pitched giggle, and opened the back door for Ben and Gran before hopping into the front seat beside Madhu.

Padam turned around to talk to them and grinned, revealing a mouth with hardly any teeth. In a sing-song voice he said, "Good golly, it is nice to have foreigners with us in our car. I see by that very fine red hat that you are from Canada and we are welcoming you."

"Thanks," Ben said. "It's our first time here."

Padam smiled. "And I am certain it will be only the first of many visits to our so-beautiful country."

"Not a chance," Ben said under his breath.

Traffic was heavy, and their taxi fought for road space with rickshaws, motor scooters, buses, exhaust-spewing trucks and pedestrians. The air around them was a haze of grey fumes; Ben saw some pedestrians wearing masks.

At the next traffic light, a beggar suddenly appeared at the side of their taxi, stretching a sinewy, not very clean arm through the taxi window toward Gran and Ben in the back seat. "*Baksheesh.* Money," the man pleaded, gesturing aggressively.

"Delhi's beggars. Do not give to them," said Padam, twisting around to roll up the back window.

The beggar was not quick enough and the window closed

on his hand. Howls of pain filled the air before Padam rolled the window down just enough to free the man's hand. The beggar fell back.

"He'll be hit!" Gran yelled as Madhu drove on.

Ben turned and saw the man scrambling to his feet.

"He is not hurt. He is unharmed," said Madhu.

"These Delhi beggars," Padam said, shaking his head. "You will learn. They are too-too pushy."

"The guy could have been run over," Ben said. He could feel himself shaking. The poor man might have been killed. He had looked poor — his shirt was ripped and filthy, and there were big scabs on his face. Ben knew they had street people at home, too, but they weren't so scary. They wouldn't be assertive enough to stick their arm right into a car. They stood on street corners with a cap in front of them, asking quietly if you'd give them money. Why had Padam crushed the man's hand like that? Was that any way to treat beggars?

Gran collapsed against the plastic seat. The incident with the beggar, the constant bleating of horns and the blasts of gas fumes were too much for her. "What have I got us into?" she moaned.

Ben felt sorry for her. "Into a bed soon, I hope, Gran. Even though it's only the middle of the afternoon here."

As the taxi pulled in front of a three-storey hotel, Gran saw there was no meter and reached into her fanny pack to pull out four bills. "I hope this is enough. Thank you very much."

"We are thanking you," said Madhu. "Now you will be needing to rest so we will be coming for you tomorrow."

"No need for you to do that. We can get a taxi when we're ready," Gran said.

Madhu gave a sideways nod of his head, "We are your drivers and we will be taking you everywhere."

"Good golly, yes," Padam said. "We are belonging to you. It is no problem."

That was the second time the men had said "no problem." Must be a common expression here, thought Ben.

On the way to the hotel desk, Ben said, "Do you know how much money you gave the taxi drivers, Gran?"

"I'm not sure," Gran said. "All the bills look the same, and right now, I'm too exhausted to figure them out."

Travelling with Gran was not going to be easy. He'd have to make sure she didn't give all their money away.

After signing the register, they made their way up an unlit stairwell to the third floor and a small room with two single beds and a much smaller bathroom.

"Smells like a leaky toilet in here," Gran said, flopping down on the bed. "But I'm too tired to care, and I can't stay awake another minute."

Ben dropped his pack on the other bed. Maybe his grandmother *was* too old for this trip.

The noise that woke Ben was like nothing he'd ever heard before — a harsh wailing sound came through the open window. The vibrating lament filled the air for several minutes and then suddenly stopped. What made a cry like that? In the silence that followed, Ben heard birds serenading the morning and Gran on the next bed snoring.

He was in Delhi, the capital of India. A country he knew nothing about. He checked his watch, which he'd set to Delhi time before the plane landed. Their flight had crossed the International Date Line, and here in Delhi it was five o'clock Wednesday morning and light outside. Counting back, it would be five o'clock on Tuesday afternoon in Vancouver. Mum and Lauren would be just sitting down to dinner while he and Gran had been catapulted half a world away and into the next day.

From the hotel window, Ben could see over the tops of trees onto a small courtyard. In the distance he saw several tall temples. Drifting up from the garden came a familiar spicy smell, a smell that reminded him of Sunday mornings when his dad baked cinnamon buns. Mornings that seemed a long time ago.

Ben reached to switch on his PlayStation. Nothing. It was dead. He looked in his backpack until he found the recharger, but the plug wouldn't fit the wall outlet. It was the wrong shape. That was odd.

He shook his grandmother's shoulder.

"What is it, Ben?" she said in a groggy voice.

"I can't get my recharger plugged in. I need to recharge my PlayStation."

"You might need an adapter."

"What's that?"

"It's a special plug. Lets you connect into their electrical system over here." She rolled over. "Just let me go back to sleep for a few minutes."

This couldn't be happening. How was he supposed to know you needed an adapter? He'd never travelled to a foreign country before. He shook his grandmother's shoulder again. This time it was harder to wake her.

"What do you want?"

"Gran, why didn't you tell me I'd need an adapter? The battery on my PlayStation has run down. I need it."

Now wide awake, his grandmother sat up. "I didn't even know you were bringing the stupid thing." She rubbed her eyes and blinked. "Well, I'm up now. Might as well get dressed and get this day started."

Ben sat on his bed. Unbelievable. No adapter meant no PlayStation. No music. No *Battlefront* for seventeen days. Just India . . . and his grandmother.

While Gran was in the bathroom, Ben dressed and called, "I'm going to send an email to Mum." He decided not to slam the door.

The desk clerk was awake and showed Ben to the computer in a room beside the front desk. Ben keyed in:

Dear Mum and Lauren

Hard 2 believe we're in Delhi. I've never seen so many people. Why didn't anyone tell me I need an adapter for my PlayStation?

Ben

Gran came downstairs and Ben followed her droopy soldier skirt to the hotel restaurant. A young waitress in a sari smiled and seated them at a table by the window. "I am guessing where you're from," she said.

"It's that baseball cap, Ben. Please take it off," Gran snapped.

Ben scowled at his grandmother and tossed the cap on the chair beside him.

"Welcome to India. I am Gita. You come from Canada! So, so far away. But I have read that it is being a very fine country."

Gita wore a starched white uniform with a blue apron. She was tiny and neat, with large eyes and a wide smile. She brought their order of poached eggs, and then pots of tea and hot chocolate and a plate of chapatis. It felt like two days since Ben had eaten. Probably was.

"You speak English," Gran said to Gita.

"Indeed, madam," she answered. "Of course, I also speak Hindi and two other languages."

"How many languages are there in India?" Gran asked.

"So many. Eighteen or more, madam. More chapatis?"

"Please," Ben said.

"Don't talk with your mouth full, Ben," Gran said.

Was his grandmother going to correct him for every little thing the whole trip?

Gran was being annoyingly chatty to the waitress. "It's lucky for us you speak English because we don't know any Hindi words," she said.

"Well," Gita said. "Here's the first one you should learn. In India when we greet someone we say *namaste* and we put our hands together in front of our chest." She demonstrated with a little forward bow.

"Our taxi drivers did that yesterday," Gran said.

"What does it mean?" Ben asked.

Gita smiled her big smile again and said. "*Namaste* means 'Greetings. I recognize the god in you.'"

"I like that," Gran said.

Back up in their room, Gran reminded Ben to take his malaria pill, then put on her goofy hat.

"You're wearing a hat, Gran. Can I put on my baseball cap?"

"Yes, because we're going out. But please put it on the right way, Ben, not backwards."

He felt like a little kid being told how to dress.

"Come on, Ben." Gran opened the door. "Let's go and find Shanti!"

Day Two

AT THE FRONT ENTRANCE of the hotel, a blanket of heat dropped over Ben and his grandmother. They stood, stunned, as the steaming air tumbled over their faces and through their clothes to their skin.

Madhu and Padam came rushing up from beside their taxi. *"Namaste,"* said Madhu, with his gentle smile and a bob of his bald head. The gap-toothed Padam repeated the greeting, bowing low.

"We didn't expect you to be here for us," Gran said.

"But of course, memsahib, we told you. We are belonging to you," Madhu said.

"Well, thank you," Gran smiled.

"How do we say 'thank you' in Hindi?" Ben asked.

"*Dhanayawada*," Padam said, slowly.

"*Dhana—ya—wada*," Ben repeated.

Gran smiled at Ben's efforts and asked the two men, "Could you please take us to the central registry office?"

"That is no problem for us, memsahib. We are knowing all the government offices." Padam bowed again and gestured toward the taxi. He closed the door after them and hopped in beside Madhu, turning around every two minutes to giggle at Gran and Ben, who were mopping their faces in the sweltering car. "Good golly, this is so exciting to be going to your most important office. Yes-yes, most important."

Ben could see that Madhu and Padam each had a role. Madhu was the serious driver and Padam, the talker with the giggle.

As the taxi headed up a wide boulevard divided by a row of trees, Ben saw dark shapes crumpled on the side of the road. As they drove closer he realized the shapes were people. The bodies were as motionless as a pile of rags; you couldn't tell if they were men or women.

"They're not dead, are they?" Ben said.

"It is possible," Madhu said, "but perhaps they are simply sleeping."

"I think that's terrible," Gran said.

"We have homeless people sleeping on the streets in the day in Vancouver, too," Ben said.

"You're right, we do," Gran replied.

Ben wondered. Madhu had said it was *possible* the people were dead. If they were dead . . . Ben pulled down the curtain in his mind that could shut out anything to do with death.

He looked out the car window, made himself guess who lived in the large houses they were passing, noting growing crowds of people rushing along the sidewalks as the taxi approached the centre of Delhi.

After a short ride, Madhu drove into a circular plaza, stopping the taxi in front of a tall building with a plaque that said CENTRAL REGISTRY OFFICE OF INDIA.

Gran counted out some bills and passed them to Padam. "I'm a little confused by the money here. Is this enough?"

"Oh, yes, memsahib," the men said together. "Most generous."

It was hard to tell from their faces if Gran had paid them too much or too little. He'd have to find out. She didn't seem to have a clue.

Inside the registry office, they hesitated. People sat on all sides of the room facing a woman at a centre desk whose heavy black eyebrows made her seem important. She listened to Gran's request, nodded and passed across some papers. "You must take a number and complete these forms. When it is your turn you will be called."

Gran and Ben sat down on the hard chairs and Gran ruffled through the forms. "All I can fill in here is Shanti's first and last name and the year she was supposed to marry,

1955." When she'd finished, all the other spaces on the form were empty.

"They want to know the names of Shanti's parents, their address and their occupations. I don't know any of that." Gran's lips were pressed tight. "With all these people, we'll be here a long time."

Ben saw his chance. "Gran, while we're waiting, you've got to let me show you about the money. I saw the exchange rates at the airport and you know I'm good at math."

Gran took a handful of pale red bills and some coins from her fanny pack and handed them to Ben.

"Look," Ben said. "These coins are paise and they are worth small amounts, like a quarter of a cent." He took one of the bills. "This ten-rupee bill one is worth about twenty-five cents. Go figure. A bill for twenty-five cents!"

All the bills were the same colour and on every one there was a picture of a man with a bald head, round black eyes and wire-rimmed glasses. Ben sorted them by denomination.

"Okay, so four of these hundred-rupee bills will be worth ten dollars. Seems like a lot of bills to be handing out, but I think I've got it."

"It's confusing," Gran said, peering at them.

"I could take care of the money, Gran."

"No, I can handle it, Ben." Gran zipped up the money in her fanny pack.

Why wouldn't she let him do it? He was old enough. He'd

be faster than she would at figuring it out. It made him feel that she didn't trust him.

Ben studied the room. Everyone else was Indian, the men in neatly pressed shirts and shorts, the women wearing colourful saris, with their long hair tied at the back of their heads. Every now and then Ben could feel himself being inspected. Around the room, people seemed curious about Gran too. Their light skin must seem very strange to the other people in the room. Next to Gran sat a woman with a small boy almost hidden in the folds of her coral-coloured sari. She had her hand on her child's back and waited patiently.

Ben watched the boy. He was about three or four years old and was sneaking peeks at Ben. The boy's serious brown eyes signalled that he thought Ben could be a creature from outer space. Ben winked at the boy, who buried his face shyly in his mother's lap. A minute later the boy lifted his head and peered at Ben again, this time with a small grin.

Ben smiled at the boy, who thought for a minute, then came out cautiously from behind his mother's sari. Ben made the *namaste* greeting. To his delight, the boy returned the greeting with a little sideways nod of his head, his small hands folded perfectly.

Before long the boy was leaning his elbows on Ben's knees as Ben showed him a clapping game he used to play with Lauren. By the time the boy was trying on Ben's baseball cap, Ben knew his name was Harish and had learned that even four-year-olds in India could speak English.

I must be really bored to be playing with a little kid, thought Ben, but almost two hours had gone by and he had to do something. The number of people ahead of them was diminishing, but slowly, and for every seat vacated, more people arrived at the door to keep the rows filled. For the tenth time that morning he thought of his PlayStation sitting out of power in the hotel room.

"So long we must be waiting here," said the boy's mother, who had introduced herself as Mrs. Rau. "And all because I must have a copy of my parents' marriage certificate for an estate settlement."

Gran told Mrs. Rau about her search for Shanti. "I wrote down everything I know on the forms, but it's probably not enough. The only other thing I know is that Shanti attended the Calcutta Senior Girls' School."

Mrs. Rau said, "You know, I also attended a girls' school. It was in the north in Darjeeling. Our school has an alumni site where we can contact fellow students. Perhaps you could use the internet to learn if your friend's Calcutta school has such a site."

"Ben could do that, he's the computer expert. But I think it might be a waste of time. The school no longer exists," Gran said.

Ben unwound Harish's arms from his legs. He could try to find Shanti on a school website. He'd do a search on the hotel computer as soon as they got back.

Ben gave Harish the loonie he still had in his pocket. Harish stared at it in amazement, tossing it from hand to hand.

Just before noon, the receptionist called Mrs. Rau's name. Harish walked backwards behind his mother, making the *namaste* sign to Ben all the way.

Shortly afterwards, Gran's number was called and they were directed into an office. A man in a blue shirt and shorts took Gran's form. He flipped over the empty pages and shook his head. "This is all the information you have for us to find this Shanti Mukherjee person?"

Gran nodded. "It is, and we've come all the way from Canada to find her."

"I welcome you to our country, Mrs. Leeson. We will search our records and do our best for you, but I am not hopeful. Please come back tomorrow afternoon." He put the paper on top of a pile on his desk and called the next number.

Maybe Uncle Bob had been right. Maybe this *was* like trying to find a camel's hair in the desert.

Outside the building, Padam and Madhu, all smiles, were waiting beside the car.

"Our hotel is not far up this main street," Ben said to Gran. "Let's walk."

"This heat is too much for me," Gran replied. "Let's have Padam and Madhu drive us." She headed for the taxi.

"You go. I'll get back myself," Ben said.

"No, I won't let you go alone! I'll come with you," she said, hurrying along the narrow sidewalk to catch up to Ben.

Padam called after them, "Goodbye for now. We will be at your hotel tomorrow to take you to the famous Red Fort. You will be liking."

"Good idea. I'd like to see a fort," Ben said to Gran as they walked. "We can't go back to the registry office until the afternoon anyway."

At the next corner, Gran and Ben were quickly surrounded by a crowd of shoving women and children. The women's saris were old and torn, their hair matted and dirty. Bedraggled, whining children who could hardly toddle clung to their mothers' skirts. One little girl had blackened teeth and big sores on her lips. The beggars stretched out their palms, calling *baksheesh, baksheesh*. They mimed hunger by raising their hands to their mouths, moaning and pleading with their eyes. An old woman put her face so close to Ben that her sour breath made him wince. "Give them some money, Gran!"

Gran ignored him and pushed to get away, but the group followed, wailing louder, grabbing at her skirt. She stumbled and Ben grabbed her arm, leading her down the sidewalk. He looked behind. They were the poorest people he'd ever seen. So much thinner and more wretched than the people who asked for money on the streets in Vancouver.

"Why didn't you give them money?" Ben asked Gran, dropping her arm. "You have lots of it."

Gran was red in the face. "I don't know what is right here. If I give rupees to some, they'll all want money."

"So what? They're poor." He turned and saw that the beggars were swamping the next couple coming along the street.

"I was frightened to be in the middle of that, Ben. I just wanted to get away. And I've heard that sometimes beggars will deliberately mutilate children and send them out to beg."

Ben followed her down the street. It was confusing and he felt uncomfortable. Maybe it was true that if you gave people money, it encouraged them to keep begging. How would you know?

Just then he heard the strange call again, the loud wavering cry he'd heard at the hotel early in the morning. It was an inhuman noise that filled the air for minutes, then stopped abruptly. Everything was weird in India.

Ahead, a wide street intersected with the road they were on and Ben saw a procession of chanting, cymbal-clashing men in orange gowns moving toward them. He was astounded to see a huge grey elephant in the middle of the crowd. The animal's ears flapped like dirty curtains, its thick trunk, criss-crossed with wrinkles, waved grandly in the air. The elephant's leathery face was painted in curlicue patterns of white and orange, and it had only one tusk, long and curved, and broken at the tip. With each giant step, looped ropes of coloured tassels swung back and forth over its humped forehead.

Without thinking, Ben moved closer to the elephant, into the middle of the noisy crowd. Orange cloth swirled around him, floating over his arms and his face, pulling him into the centre, nearer to the towering elephant. He was so close he could see grey hairs sprouting on the elephant's face. The elephant grunted and the deep reverberation travelled through Ben's body. He lifted his head to look into the beast's unblinking eyes that seemed black at first, then when Ben looked again, he saw they were the dark wet brown of thick chocolate syrup. Ancient eyes, intelligent eyes that saw right into you. Ben breathed in the strong animal smell, inhaled deeper and deeper until the rawness filled his head.

The chanting of the crowd grew louder, keeping time with the clashing cymbals, drowning out everything but the elephant. Ben stayed close beside the elephant's legs. They were like enormous grey tree trunks with huge yellowing toenails. Ben matched his footsteps to the rhythm of the elephant's lumbering steps, his ears ringing with the jangle of the bells looped around the elephant's ankles. Deep in the frenzied centre of the procession, Ben felt his mind spinning in an overpowering exhilaration.

The sharp jerk on his elbow startled Ben. He turned to see his grandmother's face. "What a crazy thing to do, Benjamin!" she was shouting.

As though from a distance, Ben called back. "Come with us!"

"Benjamin Thomas Leeson, you've completely lost your senses!"

He was grabbed and pulled onto the sidewalk. He didn't know his grandmother was so strong.

Ben shook his arm free. Why was Gran spoiling this for him? Why was she so angry?

His grandmother's voice was so shrill it hurt his ears. "What's the matter with you? You can't go wandering off like that. I need to know where you are."

"I was right here. I was safe." He watched the elephant and the orange-robed crowd continue on down the street.

"I could barely see you. You were buried in the crowd. Come on. We've got to get back to our hotel right now."

Ben trudged behind her, his face flushed, his head reeling. "I would have found my way back to the hotel, Gran."

Gran stormed along the pavement. "That's a stupid thing to say. I'm responsible for you, and you have to stay with me." She turned and glared at him. "Got it, Ben?"

Ben shrugged. It was horrible to be stuck with someone who had to have her own way about everything. And calling him stupid. She was the stupid old lady, always worrying about something. How many times in your life would you have a chance to walk in a procession beside a live elephant?

In some mysterious way Ben couldn't understand, that elephant had willed him to follow. In the middle of the crowd, being so close to the giant beast, he had forgotten where he was. Maybe it had been dumb to wander off, but he'd been completely safe.

Ben was jolted out of his thoughts. "Take off your baseball cap, Ben," Gran said as they went through the door to the hotel.

"What's wrong with it?"

"I don't like to see a hat worn inside. It's a silly thing to do."

Ben rolled his eyes as he snapped off his hat and followed his grandmother into the restaurant.

The friendly Gita was still on duty, and she suggested they might like to try pakoras. As he ate the delicious deep-fried vegetables, Ben asked Gita about the orange-gowned people and the elephant. She explained that it was a religious procession of worshippers going to a temple. "Sometimes they have an elephant with them. One of our most popular gods, Ganesh, is half-elephant and half-boy, so everyone in India loves elephants."

"There's something powerful about them," Ben said. It was hard to say what it was. Those chocolate-coloured eyes that felt as though they could see inside you? The elephants' enormous size? They were majestic.

Gran interrupted his thoughts. "I'm beat. Let's go to our room, Ben."

Upstairs, Ben plopped himself down in a chair in front of the black-and-white television.

Gran gave a big sigh. "Do you have to put your runners on the table, Ben? It's rude."

Great. Now he was rude, as well as silly for wearing his baseball cap backwards, stupid for wanting to give money to beggars, and crazy for being interested in elephants. Hadn't anyone told Gran not to use labels?

Day Three

AGAIN THE STRANGE, vibrating call woke Ben. What kind of a thing could make that noise? Now Ben thought it sounded like a goat or a cow being tortured, which made him feel weird. He got dressed and went downstairs.

The desk clerk nodded cheerfully as Ben went into the computer room.

Dear Mum and Lauren

Yesterday I saw bodies on the street and was right beside a live elephant. It's starting to bug me that Gran won't let me out of her sight.

Ben

PS. Gran snores. LOL

Then, without a pause, Ben Googled the Calcutta Senior Girls' School. He clicked on the top hit that came up, glanced over the school's home page and found the place where he could leave a message for former students. Alumni, they were called. He typed in

> To: Calcutta Senior Girls' School
>
> My grandmother, Mrs. Norah Leeson, has come from Canada to find her pen pal Shanti Mukherjee who graduated in 1952. My grandmother's name was Norah Turner when she wrote the letters. If any former students know Shanti Mukherjee, please leave a message.
>
> Thank you.
> Ben Leeson

Just as he finished, Gran popped her head into the room, telling Ben it was time for breakfast. Gita chatted with them as they ate, then wished them good luck as they headed to the entrance of the hotel. Like the day before, going through the door was like pushing through the blast from an open oven. You wanted to turn around and go back inside.

"So hot!" Gran said. "And it's only early morning."

"Look who's over there," Ben said, pointing to the shade at one side of the entrance where Madhu was leaning against the taxi and Padam was polishing the hood of the car. Ben was not surprised to see them. When they'd said "we are belonging to you," it was probably more like "you are belonging to us." It didn't matter, they were such nice guys.

"Good morning, memsahib and sahib," said Madhu, coming up to them.

"Why not call me Ben?" Ben answered.

"And call me Norah," Gran said, adjusting her fanny pack. "Memsahib makes me feel like British royalty."

"Oh, we couldn't do that, memsahib," said Padam. "You are being so very old and both of you are being our honoured guests."

Madhu said, "We will call you Norah memsahib and Ben sahib." Padam nodded enthusiastically with a high-pitched giggle. "Today, we will be seeing the Red Fort. You must hop-hop into our so-shiny vehicle!"

It must have rained during the night. The dust on the road was hard-packed, and the smell, harsh and musky in Ben's nose. He leaned forward as they drove. "Can I ask you something?"

"Of course, Ben sahib," the men answered together.

"There's a loud call I keep hearing. Usually in the mornings, but yesterday I heard it in the day too. Sort of like a wailing. Do you know what it is?"

"Indeed, yes, we do," Madhu answered. "It will be the muezzins calling Muslim people to prayer at the mosques. Five times a day they call."

"Now you are knowing," Padam added. "The muezzins have strong voices which are being sent by so-loud loudspeakers to reach every part of the city."

"Watch, I will turn here and will be driving past the Jama

Masjid, India's largest mosque," Madhu said, turning a corner. "There, you see the grand mosque?"

Ben saw a long row of steps leading to a massive stone building, bigger than the stadium in Vancouver, with two tall towers at either side.

"The muezzins call from the tops of those towers called minarets," Madhu said, "and believe it or not, twenty-five thousand worshippers can fit into the courtyard."

"Do Muslims really pray five times a day?" Ben asked.

"Indeed, they do try wherever they are," Padam answered. "But only men can go inside the mosque. See those women on the street wearing black robes? They are Muslim women. See how their heads and faces are covered? It is to be protecting the modesty of the Muslim women."

"I thought people in India were all Hindus," Ben said.

"Oh my no, we have a mixed curry of religions here in India! Hindus, Muslims, Sikhs, Jews and Christians." Padam's grin was so wide that Ben discovered there were still three teeth left in his mouth.

Huge mosques, muezzins calling five times a day, worshippers walking with elephants down the streets. Religion was everywhere in India.

Madhu stopped the taxi beside a red stone wall. "We are here now at the Red Fort which is called 'red' because of the colour of the stone used to build it."

Along with a stream of tourists, the four of them went through the tall gate into a courtyard with a large lotus-shaped pool. "Come now," Madhu said. "You must see where water used to flow in a river of marble past the private rooms of Emperor Shah Jehan's wives."

"Did you say wives?" Gran asked.

"Only four, Norah memsahib. Oo la la!" said Padam, his shoulders shaking with squeaky laughter.

This made Gran and Madhu laugh. In spite of himself, Ben laughed too.

Gran kept turning around to watch the Indian women walking beside them. "All those women in their colourful saris! They're like brilliant butterflies weaving in and out of the crowd," she said.

"Hindu women look truly beautiful in their saris," Madhu answered. "Come now and let me show you where the fort's walls are covered in precious jewels in designs of birds and flowers."

Ben followed behind. Women like butterflies? Precious jewels? This was supposed to be a fort. Didn't they fight battles in forts?

"It's so peaceful here. I could stay forever if it wasn't so hot," Gran said.

Too peaceful. Too boring. Ben felt like telling his grandmother: You stay. I'm going back to Canada. The oohs and ahhs she kept making were what you'd expect travelling with an old lady in a droopy skirt and a hat with holes in it. If he could think of a way to dump her and go off on his own, he just might. Ben looked up to see Madhu signalling him.

"Come with us now to the viewing balcony to see the magicians," Madhu said, leading them up a short flight of stairs.

Magicians. That was more like it. He'd stick around for a while.

Tourists had gathered in the full sun on the low balcony to see the show. Below the balcony a man lay on the grass with the magician standing over him. Slowly, with each lift of the magician's wand, the man began to rise off the grass. Higher and higher, as though on an invisible bed, he floated in the air. He wobbled a bit, and then, seemingly in a trance, steadied, suspended almost two metres off the ground.

"Ohh," breathed the crowd.

That was a cool trick. Was the man held up with ropes or were mirrors hiding some kind of support? As if in answer to the questions in Ben's head, the magician began to sweep the wand over, above and below the levitating man to show there were no ropes or trick boxes. Ben joined the crowd as it burst into applause. The magician bowed, waited for people to throw down coins, and then waved his wand to bring the man's body slowly back down to the ground.

The man sat up, shook himself as though coming out of a dream, then stood and began to pick up coins.

"Can you believe what we just saw, Gran!" Ben said. "This is more like it. I was so amazed I forgot to take pictures."

"It's got to be a trick, but a darn good one," Gran said, handing Ben some coins to throw down.

"Tut-tut. It was no trick, Norah memsahib," interjected Padam. "Never must you be saying you don't believe in magic."

Ben wondered. Something you'd seen with your own eyes had to be real. But how could a man levitate in the air with no wires or tricks?

Ben looked at his grandmother. Despite the holes in her hat, perspiration was glistening on her cheeks and around her neck. Her lipstick had melted and was running into the lines around her mouth. Sweat stung his own eyes. He checked the thermometer that he had put on his daypack. Forty-one degrees! They were all cooking.

Madhu said, "Next you must be watching one of our cobra charmers."

Cobras! Ben forgot the heat. This place was unreal.

A man wearing a high turban and ballooning striped pants took his place just a few metres below them. He carried a short flute and a large woven basket. The man placed the basket on the ground, opened the lid and began to play a reedy tune, dipping the flute toward the open basket, then swirling it up to the sky. Slowly, a large black and yellow cobra with a frilled hood emerged from the basket. The snake wove higher and higher, rising closer to the flute. The crowd gasped and when the cobra struck out at the flute player Gran shrieked and clutched Ben.

She was breathing fast and her face was ashen. "I can't stay. Take me away."

"Do not worry," said Madhu. "We are safe up here, Norah memsahib. Hold my arm."

Ben couldn't move his eyes from the scene below. Weaving in time to the music, the snake twisted and lunged toward the crowd. They were close enough for Ben to see the flick of its forked tongue, and this time he remembered to take a photograph.

Gran screamed. *"Get me away from here. Please!"* She turned her face and drooped against Madhu's arm.

"He's not finished yet, he's doing more. Let's stay," Ben whispered.

"We must be taking your grandmother out of the heat. Come." Madhu and Padam stood on either side of Gran, each of them holding an arm, and almost hoisted her down the stairs.

Ben desperately wanted to see the rest of the act. He'd only ever seen snakes in zoos, where they just lay around in a display case without moving. But it *was* hot. His hair was dripping wet under his cap and his legs were sweating in his jeans. His mother had been right when she told him he should buy shorts. He'd noticed that most Indian men, including Padam and Madhu, wore cotton shorts. Reluctantly, he followed to join the others in the shade by a stone fountain.

Gran was sitting down, mopping her face. "I'm sorry I made a fuss," she said. "Snakes are the one thing I'm deathly scared of."

Madhu said, "You must not worry. We are all different. I can see that Norah memsahib loves marble and precious stones and Ben sahib prefers the cleverness of our magicians and our snake charmers."

Ben stood by himself, trying to understand what he'd seen. There was an expression, "seeing is believing." He knew what he'd seen with his own eyes. Did that mean he believed a man could levitate and a snake could be made to dance to music? In Canada people would laugh at these things. But this was India, and he was no longer sure what to believe.

After a cold drink Gran said she felt better and would like to explore the market across the street.

"This is called the Chandni Chowk," Madhu told them. "It is said that anything stolen in New Delhi turns up here within twenty-four hours."

Padam rushed to explain. "You must not think ill of our country. Not everything is stolen." He waved his hands in the air. "My goody-goodness it is not."

Ben had never seen such a crush of humanity in his life. Streams of men and women brushed past them on the road in both directions. On either side, stalls were piled with radios, television sets, carpets and leather suitcases. Counters were laden with gold jewellery, stone pots, brass statues; further along were rows of coloured powders and sacks of chilies and lentils. The air smelled of a confusing blend of sharp spices, cooked food and body sweat, his own included.

Then, without warning, the noise of the street seemed to

drop away, and Ben was staring at a stone statue a little taller than he was, on a platform across the road. He had to get closer.

Madhu scurried after him. "Ben sahib, this is our popular god, Ganesh. The elephant boy we call him. Children are asking Ganesh to help when they have some difficulty."

It was a happy-looking god. The plump elephant's face had a broad smile. Its long trunk fell over the round belly and the pudgy crossed legs of a seated boy. The elephant god had four arms and long ears. Madhu said, "Ganesh has big ears so he can listen when children talk to him. Look carefully. See one of his hands holds a round cake? This god is fond of sweets."

"Just like my grandmother," Ben laughed.

Ben ran his hand down the elephant's curving trunk. It was hot from the sun and strangely smooth. It felt almost human. What was it about these Indian elephants? He had the same feeling yesterday at the street parade when he'd been drawn to the live elephant. This was only a statue, but it was pulling him powerfully.

"You like our Ganesh, Ben sahib?" Madhu asked.

Ben kept his hand on the warm trunk and turned to answer. "What kid wouldn't like a god who listens to children?"

"We must go now, Ben sahib," Madhu said. Once again, Ben wasn't ready to leave but he knew he had to go with Madhu back to the taxi where Gran and Padam were waiting. It would be time for them to return to the registry office.

At the door to the office building, Gran thanked the two men. She hesitated and then asked Ben if he'd sort out the money to pay them. "Who's this man on the bills?" Ben asked as he handed the rupees to Madhu.

"That is our beloved Mahatma Gandhi," Madhu said. "India's great spiritual leader during our independence. This humble man travelled everywhere wearing only a simple cotton loincloth we call a dhoti. Our leader is renowned for telling us we must show patience and persistence."

Padam interrupted in his squeaky voice, "Patience and persistence. Qualities I strive to reach for myself."

Madhu added, "And seldom achieve!" The two men nudged each other and giggled.

Gran looked as though she was feeling better but her hat was tilted at a funny angle. She straightened it and said, "We might be a long time at the registry office today, and I don't want to keep you waiting. Could we take you to dinner tonight to say a proper thank you?"

Madhu beamed. "Thank you indeed, Norah memsahib. We are being honoured and will come to your hotel at seven this evening."

Ben wished his friend Mac was around to bring along, but at least eating with these two drivers would be more fun than eating alone with Gran.

The registry waiting room was as crowded as it had been the day before. Ben took a number from the same bushy-browed receptionist at the front desk and they found the last two empty seats along the wall.

Number 16 had just been called. Ben held number 52 in his hand. He looked around. There was no window in the stuffy room. It felt as though the hot air from other people's breathing was being recycled up his nose. He tried to take shallow inhalations so the stale air didn't reach his lungs. It didn't seem to bother Gran, who had opened her guidebook and was reading. Ben wished little Harish were here to help pass the time. Even better, if he could lose himself in a game on his PSP. He watched flies chase each other against the smudged wall. An old man across the room sneezed seven times, then pulled himself together and sneezed twice more.

Ben turned his thoughts to the man levitating above the ground at the Red Fort. Was that real or did you have to believe in some kind of magic like Padam had said? Ben was mad at himself for not taking a picture, but at least he had one of the cobra taken before Gran had started to scream.

That statue of Ganesh made him wonder why Hindus had a god with an elephant's head on a boy's body. Mac would think India was right over the top when he heard about that.

Number 28 was called, and a fat woman carrying a crying baby went up to the desk. Gran lifted her head from the guidebook. "Listen to this, Ben. I'm reading the story of Ganesh."

"I was just thinking about him," Ben said.

"The story says that the god Shiva went away to travel the world, leaving his wife Parvati and his infant son behind. His wife waited for him and gave instructions that no other man was to be allowed to enter her room. Shiva travelled for a long time and when he returned, he rushed to see Parvati, but a young man blocked the door. Shiva was so mad he cut off the man's head, but then Parvati told him he'd cut off his own son's head. His son had grown up while Shiva was away."

Gran read on, "Shiva felt terrible at his mistake and swore he would make their son whole. He promised to find a head for his son from the first living thing he saw. The first thing he saw was an elephant, and true to his word, Shiva cut off the elephant's head and put it on his son's body."

"Now they have a god who is half-boy, half-elephant," Ben said. "Unreal!"

"Number 57."

Ben and Gran leapt to their feet.

"Good day, Madam Leeson," said the blue-shirted man at his office desk. "Happy news. We have been fortunate to find some information for you."

He held a paper out to Gran. "It seems Miss Shanti Mukherjee was married in 1955 from her parents' home in Agra. You will see I have written the address where she lived with her parents. 187 B Station Cross Road in Agra."

"That's wonderful! I've never had a home address, only her school address," Gran said. "Where is Agra?"

"About two hundred kilometres from here. Agra is the home of the famous Taj Mahal. It will be possible for you see it and find your friend's family at the same time."

"Thank you, thank you," Gran said.

"Good luck and *namaste*."

Ben said *namaste* and made the hand gesture in return. Good. Now they'd be able to see more sights in India.

Gran put the paper in her fanny pack. "What luck! An address for Shanti's parents. They'd be very old now, but if they're alive, they'll know where Shanti is for sure."

As they headed out into the blistering air, Gran said, "Imagine Shanti's family living in the same city as the Taj Mahal! We'll go to Agra tomorrow." She reached over and put her arm around Ben's shoulders.

Ben ducked out from under her arm. He wished she wouldn't do that. "Okay with me. How about celebrating with a ride in one of those auto-rickshaws?"

Before his grandmother could object, Ben waved at a driver who immediately swerved to the curb, pulling his yellow and green vehicle to a shuddering stop beside them. The auto-rickshaw had one wheel in front and two in the back, above a small, noisy engine. Behind the driver was a plastic seat with a curved canvas hood. Ben jumped in first, not waiting for approval from Gran.

"Well, why not?" Gran said climbing in behind him. Nervously, she gave the driver the name of their hotel.

It was a wild ride. The driver steered the rickshaw on a reckless course, threading his way like a buzzing yellow bee between bigger cars and buses, while the engine droned and sputtered, the vibrations from the old engine rattling the teeth in Ben's head. Gran held onto a bar at her side, but was hurled against Ben and back again as their driver whizzed past every vehicle on the road.

Ben got out first. "That was a lot more fun than a taxi, Gran. Let's do it again!"

"Please, not today," said Gran, fanning her face with her hat. I'm going upstairs for a long rest." Ben could see that her legs were shaking under her skirt.

He asked if he could borrow the guidebook and found a seat in the hotel garden. He studied the trumpeting elephant on the cover. Now he'd seen a real elephant. A striking cobra too. And an elephant boy-god. It had been quite a day. He opened the book to read the story about Ganesh again.

Right at seven, Madhu and Padam showed up at the entrance to the hotel. They wore freshly pressed shirts and long pants and announced they had chosen a restaurant in an area that Padam said was "posh-posh." Soon they were in the taxi, barrelling down the road through a row of large hotels.

As they walked up to the door of the restaurant, Gran frowned at Ben and said under her breath, "Benjamin. Hat!" Ben gave her a look and took off his baseball cap. It didn't seem to bother Madhu or Padam, who had both admired it at the Red Fort.

The restaurant had tables covered with white cloths, and sparkling chandeliers hung from the high ceiling. Madhu explained in his quiet way that he was a vegetarian and Padam was not, so they had chosen a restaurant that served a buffet meal with choices for everyone.

Padam bounced around in his seat as the waiter handed him a linen napkin. "We are most excited. We are not usually eating with foreigners like yourselves."

They filled their plates from the long table. Padam suggested Ben try the chicken and the special spinach and cheese dish. Madhu loaded his plate with all sorts of vegetable dishes, rice and dhal, which he said was a sauce made of lentils.

Ben checked the table. There were no forks. He watched in disbelief as the two men began to pick up fingerfuls of food with their hands.

"I can see you are not knowing the Indian way," Padam said. "Watch me. You must be holding your fingers together to make a little scoop."

Gran had her fingers in the food. Obviously this was what you did here. Ben reached to pick up the food on his plate, but before he got any to his mouth, Padam interrupted. "Please, only your right hand, sahib."

"Why? I'm left-handed," Ben said.

"Because in India the left hand is used to perform certain bathroom cleaning rituals," Padam answered.

Gross. Didn't they have toilet paper in this country? Maybe they meant that the left hand was used to hold toilet paper? Ben decided not to think about it.

It felt awkward using his right hand; most of the food slid in a sloppy pile on the table. Gran was having the same trouble.

"Watch us," Padam said. "Watch how we use the rotis." He

held up a circle of bread so thin you could almost see through it. "You must laugh when you are knowing we call it hand-kerchief bread."

Copying them, Ben and Gran curled the bread and used it like a ladle.

Madhu nodded in approval. "You like our tandoori chicken? It is a specialty here in the north. It is marinated overnight in yogurt and spices, then it is being cooked in a clay oven."

"So good," Ben answered. His next mouthful was a potato cake in a spicy sauce that felt deliciously hot all the way down his throat.

Even with most of his teeth missing, Padam managed to eat two heaped platefuls of food, talking and giggling through the meal.

Gran chose two desserts: a tapioca dish with sliced mangoes and three sweet cakes.

The men showed Ben and Gran where to wash their hands at a sink to one side of the dining room. Then they all sat back down to eat another dessert: Indian ice cream full of pistachio nuts that luckily was served with a small ladle.

"Tell us about yourselves," Gran said. "Do you have families?"

"Yes, we are both living with our parents. Like you, they are so old, and we must be taking care of them. Our money from driving the taxi we give to them," Madhu said.

Padam nodded. "Madhu and I have been friends since

our school days, just like you and your Indian friend, Norah memsahib."

"I'm excited that maybe I'll find Shanti now that I have the address of her parents in Agra," Gran said.

"To go to Agra, how are you doing that?" Padam asked.

Gran was eyeing the buffet. Probably trying to decide if she should try another piece of cake. Apparently, she decided not to. "We'll find out in the morning. I understand there is a bus."

"Norah memsahib, I have a very good thought," Madhu said, leaning over the table. "Would you consent to have us drive you to Agra? It is only a five-hour drive and we could be telling you about many sights along the way."

"Awesome idea! Let's do it, Gran," Ben exclaimed.

Padam was squirming with excitement. "We will charge you the minimum, cheap-cheap, and you will have the comfort of our taxi, not being stuffed into a hot bus with many other so-noisy people."

It was settled. The taxi would pick them up at eight in the morning. The two men thanked them over and over for the dinner when they returned to the hotel.

Inside the lobby, Ben nodded to the night clerk and turned to go into the computer room.

"Don't bother with email tonight," Gran said. "We have to pack and get to bed for an early start."

It seemed as though she was trying to rule him every minute of the day. "I just want to see if Mum and Lauren have sent a message," he called on his way out.

"Hurry up then," Gran said.

When he returned to the bedroom, Ben went to turn on the television. Gran was rolling clothes to put into her backpack. "No television tonight, Ben. Get packing."

Ben plunked himself down in a chair. He hated the way she bossed him around, but he got up and began to stuff his clothes in his pack, thinking about the road trip the next day. "I like being with Padam and Madhu, don't you? They're funny. The way Padam jokes around reminds me of Dad."

"Padam isn't like your father, Ben. Are you finished packing?"

Something snapped in Ben. "Stop nagging me! Take off your hat, Ben. Don't talk with your mouth full, Ben. No television, Ben. Get packing, Ben . . ."

"Come on," Gran interrupted. "Stop feeling sorry for yourself." She went closer to Ben, looking as though she intended to give him another hug.

Ben stepped back and said, "I *do* feel sorry for myself. No other kid I know has a father who died."

"You are not the only one to miss your father, Ben. Lauren lost a father too, and I lost my only son. Your mother lost her life partner. Her life is turned upside down. Do you ever take time to think of her?"

"Sure I think of my mother."

"Ben, your loss is no greater than ours. I'd hoped this trip would teach you to think about other people."

"All I can think of is *you* . . . nagging me." Just before he slammed the bathroom door, Ben called, "By the way, Mum sent an email. She says she hopes we're having fun together."

Day Four

BEN WOKE TO HEAR his grandmother singing. It sounded like the lame song "Somewhere over the Rainbow." She must be in a happier mood. She came over to his bed and perched on the edge, smiling down at him. "I'm sorry about last night, Ben."

This was a change. He was the one who usually had to apologize.

Gran went on. "I was exhausted. I get cranky when I'm tired after a long day. I'll try to do better."

She seemed so ashamed that Ben said, "It's okay, Gran. I was crabby too. I know I'm not the only one who misses Dad, but sometimes I just can't believe I'll never see him again."

"I can't believe it either, but I guess I'm lucky. I can see you and be reminded of him."

"In some ways you remind me of him too, Gran." Ben grinned at his grandmother. It was true, in some ways she did, but one sure thing was that his dad would never have owned a hat like hers.

After a quick breakfast during which they said goodbye to Gita, Ben took their backpacks outside, where Padam and Madhu waited beside the taxi, excited and giggling, ready for the trip.

Gran and Ben got into the back seat. "No seatbelts, I guess," Gran said.

"It is being no problem," Madhu said, not in the least defensive. "You will be seeing how safely our fine car travels on the road to Agra."

No problem. No problem. Seems that was the Indian way.

Gran asked, "I don't suppose your car has air conditioning?"

"We most certainly do, Norah memsahib." Padam turned in his seat to answer. "Simply roll down your window and the air is conditioned in an extremely fine way!" He giggled crazily at his own joke.

Gran smiled at Ben. "I shouldn't have asked."

"No problem," Ben said. Now he was saying it too.

They drove for an hour in heavy traffic through the crowded outskirts of Delhi. Mile after mile, crowded, broken-down dwellings stretched in rows back from the road: tin shacks, houses built of wooden crates, open shelters with makeshift roofs of tar paper and cardboard. Women in worn saris stood in the doorways with children playing in the dirt around them. One boy, about Ben's age with long skinny legs, sat on a crumbling roof waving at the traffic. Before Ben could wave back, Padam had sped past. The acrid smell of smoldering garbage came with them in the taxi like a reeking stowaway.

"I had no idea people lived like that," Gran said.

"Not all people do, but we have too-too many people in India now," Padam said. "Over one billion."

One billion people! And this was where many of them had to live. What a terrible place for that poor boy to grow up.

They came to a two-lane highway heading south where a crooked wooden sign read: To Agra 206 km. Their small taxi shared the road with an endless stream of larger vehicles. Local buses were crammed with people peering out the small windows, clinging to the sides and riding on the roof beside luggage tied down with ropes. Transport trucks, top heavy with full loads of cabbages and melons, careened all over the road, horns honking. Huge oil trucks roared by, their cabs decorated with dangling tassels of red pom-poms, looking as though they belonged to a circus.

The scariest part of the trip was when drivers decided to play "chicken." A truck would speed toward their taxi in the middle of the road, faster and closer, neither vehicle giving up the centre position. Ben could see that the first to swerve to the side of the road was "chicken." Invariably Madhu gave way, but usually his pride held until the last minute, by which time Gran would be gasping, her hands over her eyes. This made Padam and Ben giggle again. Ben stopped laughing when they drove past the rusty wrecks of two transport trucks overturned at the side of the road.

Just after Madhu had swerved to miss a bus, a scrawny cow chose to amble across the road. Every vehicle in both directions came to a sudden screeching halt.

"You know we cannot harm a cow. They are sacred to Hindus and they must die a natural death," Padam said.

While they waited for the cow to cross, Madhu turned around in his seat to tell his story. "Here is what happened once on this very road. A bus driver accidentally hit a cow. It was not his fault, for the cow simply strolled in front of the bus. However, the cow most sadly died and all the villagers arrived from nearby and threatened to kill the driver."

Ben was amazed to hear this. "Because he accidentally killed a cow?"

"Indeed. The poor man was never allowed to drive this road again because the village people have vowed to be watching for him. I know the man; he drives in the north now."

"Why are cows so holy anyway?" Ben asked.

"Because our supreme Hindu god, Lord Krishna, deemed it so. You see, cows are providing milk and butter for our families and also dung which is being made into patties for cooking fuel."

The cow ambled slowly onto the roadside, and the cars sped off. What a trip! No seatbelts. Playing "chicken" with truck drivers. Cows wandering on the road. Ben wondered how he'd ever explain India to anyone at home.

The temperature inside the car was rising, but when Gran opened the window, a blast of foul exhaust from passing trucks poured into the car. "I feel a little sick. Can we stop to stretch our legs?" she asked.

"Norah memsahib, this is no problem," Madhu said. "We will stop at the next village."

Before long, Madhu pulled the taxi up beside four small shacks. At the side of the road, women and children squatted on the ground, the women's fingers scratching for lice in their children's matted hair.

As he got out of the car Ben realized his jeans were stuck to the back of his legs, and he wished for the hundredth time in four days that he'd brought a pair of shorts. Then he had an idea. While Gran went toward the side of the road where a wooden shack had "Toilet" written above the door, Ben opened the scissors on his pocket knife and cut first one leg of his jeans and then the other just above the knee. It wasn't easy. The jeans were tough to cut, and he didn't get the legs exactly even, but he'd be cooler.

Ben found the men's toilet, which was two pieces of wood on either side of a hole. The hole sat over a small creek.

When they met outside, Ben asked Gran, "What was the women's toilet like?"

"I'd like to say it was no problem, but I can't," was the answer from his grim-faced grandmother. Then she noticed his cut-off jeans. "I see you took things into your own hands."

Ben looked over to the bench where he'd left the pant legs. They were gone. Maybe someone would use the fabric to sew pants for a child.

As they made their way to stalls where Padam and Madhu were talking to the village men, Gran stepped in the centre of a wet cow patty. Ben heard her mutter "Something . . . something holy cows."

"Welcome to India," Ben joked.

"Not funny," Gran said, wiping her shoe on the ground. "I need to scrape this mess off."

Ben lined up to buy water and came back with two cans of warm orange soda. "Sorry, Gran. No bottled water here."

Padam came back with bananas and a package of cookies. They sat in the shade of a large tree and Ben passed his banana peel to two scrawny goats nudging at his bare knees for handouts.

"Ben sahib," Madhu said, quietly at his side. "I am most sorry to mention this but you have been using your left hand to hold the fruit. You must be remembering this is not good in our country."

Ben realized he'd had the soda and a cookie in his right hand but had used his left to hold the banana. "Sorry. I forgot."

"Norah memsahib, watch out!" Madhu called.

An agile monkey had swung by its tail from the tree above them, making a grab for Gran's banana.

"Those monkeys, they are terrible thieves!" laughed Padam, shooing the monkey away.

Ben glanced up. The tree was alive with monkeys. Emboldened by the sight of bananas they were scrambling down from the branches, stretching out their hairy arms to swipe at the food. Gran and Ben leapt from their seats and backed away, trying to hang onto their drinks, the bananas and cookies in their right hands.

On the way back to the car, Gran missed seeing another deposit of cow dung and managed to have both runners freshly anointed. "I can't believe this," she said in distress as Madhu rushed to help her wipe them at the side of the road.

"No problem," Padam said when they were settled in the car. "Here in India we are saying it is good luck to step in a gift from our sacred cows."

"You've got to be the luckiest person around here today, Gran," joked Ben, relieved that Gran could stop sniffing at her shoes long enough to laugh.

"And you, Ben sahib," Padam said, turning around in his seat to see Ben's pants. "You are looking most extremely smart now."

"*Dhanayawada*," Ben said. "Did I say 'thank you' the right way?"

"Most extremely correct," beamed Padam.

An hour later, they were stalled by another cow who'd

decided, despite the raucous honking of horns, to fall asleep in the middle of the road.

"It is no problem," Madhu said, waiting until some men prodded the cow gently and she meandered to the side of the road. No problem for anything it seemed.

Padam pointed to temple spires in the distance. "It is said that one day when Shiva, the destroyer god, was angry he cut up his wife. Where he threw the pieces of her body there are now temples."

"These Hindu gods are something else!" Ben said. He checked Gran to see if she thought this story was a bit gruesome, but her head was bent, sniffing at her runners, and she didn't seem to hear him.

"If you like, we will take you inside the courtyard of a temple," Madhu offered. "But first we will stop for some lunch."

"Great idea," Ben said. The cookies were so stale he'd eaten only one.

Shortly, Madhu pulled the car up to the shady yard of a roadside restaurant with rows of benches and tables. Steaming pots of food were cooking on smoky fires. Gran and Ben found a seat, making sure it was not under a tree. An old woman appeared and put a flat banana leaf as a plate in front of them; then she dished out a delicious potato and carrot curry. Ben was becoming quite good at using his right hand as a scoop, unlike Gran, who still dropped food down the front of her shirt.

"This food was boiled so it's probably safe to eat," Gran said, "but now I'm too hungry to worry."

"No problem," said Padam. "I give my personal guarantee."

"It's delicious!" Ben said, brushing away a fly.

They purchased mangoes, oranges and bananas for the rest of the trip, which was taking much longer than Madhu had predicted the night before.

"This pocket knife has come in handy today, Gran," Ben said, as he grabbed a mango to peel.

They drove for another hour, once passing a tall ungainly camel led by a man and his wife. The camel's long neck was decorated with flowers and ribbons, and two small children sat dangling their short legs over the camel's hump as the creature meandered along on spindly legs.

Madhu announced that they were close to a large Shiva temple where foreigners would be allowed into the outer courtyard, but not inside where the statue of the god was kept.

He pulled up to the parking area and they walked through a gateway painted with pictures of gods and demons. Ahead was a tapered stone tower covered in sculptured figures.

"This temple is dedicated to the god Shiva," Padam said. "Shiva's sanctuary is deep inside the temple and only devout Hindus are allowed to see him."

"Wicked!" Ben said. "You mean the guy who tossed pieces of his wife's body all around?"

"Benjamin!" said Gran.

"That's what Padam said, Gran."

Many people waiting to enter the temple seemed tired and poor. One man was naked except for a white dhoti. His body was smeared in white ash and his matted hair fell to the top of his knobby knees. He had a red mark in the centre of his forehead and he shuffled along with a cane, carrying a cloth bag over his shoulder.

"He is a sadhu, a holy man who travels the country with all his worldly goods in that small satchel," Madhu said. "People give him money and he will always find food at temples such as this."

Over the noise of the crowd, Ben heard a band.

"Oh, we are most-most fortunate today," Padam said, his high voice even squeakier in his excitement. "There is to be a wedding and you will see the arrival of the bride and groom."

Just then, a white horse decorated with red ribbons entered the courtyard. Seated on the horse was a young man dressed in white with a high Rajah-style turban on his head. A crowd of about thirty men and boys gathered around him.

"The groom and his supporters," Madhu said.

Next, a large van pulled up and a group of women flowed out, surrounding a young dark-haired bride. She wore flowers in her hair and was dressed in a red sari with rows of gold necklaces and bracelets.

"The Brahmin priest will be blessing them and wishing them many children. But come now," Madhu said. "We must return to our trusty car and make our way to Agra. We have an hour still to go."

As the taxi headed onto the road again, Ben said, "I'd like to go inside a temple sometime. Are there temples for other gods?"

"Oh, my word yes! And goddesses too," Padam said in his giggly voice. "The most frightening of all the goddesses is Black Kali, the goddess of destruction and death. She has many arms and weapons and always she is demanding sacrifices. I saw her in a temple, and now I am too-too frightened ever since."

Ben stared out the window. A goddess who demanded sacrifices? India was epic. His thoughts drifted along as the miles passed when suddenly there was a loud bang and the car veered to the right. Gran had fallen asleep and woke with a start. "What's that? What happened?"

Padam jumped out. "Flat tire. Oh, good golly, we are having a flattened tire!"

Madhu scratched his bald head and peered at the rear tire, which had collapsed over the rim. "No problem," Madhu said. "We have a spare in the boot."

Ben had never seen a tire worn so thin; in fact, there was no tread at all. Padam rushed excitedly around, but it was Madhu who calmly jacked up the car and replaced the tire. Ben went over to Gran, who was sitting at the side of the road. "I'm not sure we'll make it to Agra, Gran. There's no tread on the new tire either."

"This five-hour trip is taking all day," Gran said. "I just want to get there alive."

It was late afternoon when they finally reached Agra. Madhu stopped at the first hotel they came to. Over the door of the Hotel Rama, flashed a neon sign: THREE STAR DELUX! AIR-CONDITIONING!

Padam and Madhu offered to stay to drive them back to Delhi, but Gran said it might take several days to find Shanti. She insisted they return to work in Delhi. "Thank you so much, kind friends," Gran said. "Such a long day for you. It will be after midnight before you get back."

"Our simple lives are rich-rich for spending this long day with Norah memsahib and Ben sahib," Madhu said.

Gran passed the money from her fanny pack to Ben so he could pay Madhu. Ben gave Madhu an amount that seemed fair. Without saying any more about it, Gran had started letting Ben handle all their money. The two men thanked them and bowed low in respectful *namastes*. Ben and Gran returned the blessing and watched the small grey car turn back toward the highway.

"It's sad to say goodbye to Padam and Madhu, isn't it?" Ben said.

Gran nodded as she shifted her backpack. "That's the way travel is. You connect with people and never see them again. Every time I think of the Red Fort I'll think of Padam giggling about Shah Jehan's wives."

"Every time I think of that pit for a toilet, I'll remember this trip," Ben said.

The Hotel Rama desk clerk lifted his head from reading

the newspaper and signed them in. The lobby was shabby, and the room with twin beds wasn't clean, but they were too weary to care.

"What a day," Gran said, leaving her smelly runners outside the door. She tossed her socks in the corner and plopped down on one of the beds. "First thing in the morning we'll look for Shanti's parents."

No dinner tonight, Ben thought. He ate two of the leftover bananas. But when he tried to get the television to work, the screen flashed in a scramble of black-and-white lines.

"I'll see if the man at the desk can fix it. Be right back," Ben said.

"Of course, sir," the desk clerk said. "We will be sending up our repair man."

Ben went to the front door and scanned the street. In the darkness a non-stop crowd of rickshaws and motorbikes sped by. He looked for a sign advertising internet service, but didn't see one. He'd wait to email until after they'd found Shanti's house. It would be good to have some real news. Maybe someone would have responded on the school site too.

Ben went back up to the bedroom, and after a long wait, answered a timid knock at the door. An old man stood with a toilet plunger in his hand. "I have come, sir, to fix for you."

"But it's the television that's broken!" Ben said.

The man waved the plunger in the air. "Oh, sir, but I am not knowing about television. In the morning you will be having a man who is the expert."

Ben laughed with Gran. "Do you suppose he thought we'd use the plunger like an ear trumpet?"

"He did seem sorry he couldn't help us," Gran said. She was reading on her bed. "Ben, it's stuffy in here. That ceiling fan must be what they call air-conditioning. Would you please turn it on?"

Ben flicked the switch on the wall, but the wooden blades didn't move. "Some three-star hotel!" Ben said. "I'll try the front desk again."

I'd better make it clear, Ben thought as approached the desk clerk. He moved his arms in a circle over his head. "Broken fan. It's too hot."

The desk clerk sighed. "Sir, I understand, and now we will be sending our fine repair man up most hastily indeed."

Another long wait, then Ben opened the door to the same old man, this time with a fly swatter in his hand. "I am here to fix," he said.

Ben could hear Gran stifling her laughter behind him.

"But it's the fan." Ben pointed to the ceiling. "The fly swatter won't do much good."

The poor man looked stricken and backed away. "Most sorry, sir. Extremely most sorry." He rushed back down the hallway, the fly swatter hanging uselessly in his hand.

Gran and Ben lay on their beds and laughed until their stomachs ached.

Out of the corner of his eye, Ben saw a scurry of something moving in the corner of the room. Then another movement. Cockroaches. Better not tell Gran. She'd spaz for sure.

"Look at the sign over the door, Gran." Ben pointed to a crudely lettered message in a frame.

HOTEL RAMA
It's more than a hotel, it's an experience

"They're right about that," Ben said as he joined Gran in another burst of laughter. He laughed so hard he forgot all about the long drive and the terrible toilets and how far they were from anyone they knew. He even forgot how much his grandmother had been annoying him.

Day Five

THE HOTEL RAMA appeared even drearier in the morning than it had at night. Ben agreed with Gran that they couldn't trust the empty restaurant near the front door. They crossed the street to another restaurant and ordered what everyone else seemed to be having for breakfast. The parathas turned out to be steaming hot bread pockets stuffed with potatoes and onions. "Better than porridge any day," Ben said.

As they sat at the table waiting for the server to bring tea, Ben said, "You know, Gran. You've been handing the money over to me to pay. Why not let me keep it?"

"I do find the whole money thing a hassle, but I don't know, Ben."

"I can do it. I'd like to. You can keep the bank card."

"I've got over three hundred dollars in rupees here, Ben. It's too much responsibility for a boy your age."

"I *need* responsibility. I told Mum I'd help you."

She was so frustrating. A grandmother should know that thirteen-year-olds need to be challenged. How could he persuade her that it would be easy for him to take care of the money? Maybe if he tried to look older.

Gran was watching him. Ben adjusted his expression, putting what he hoped was a serious slant on his mouth, a knowing frown across his eyebrows. He hoped he looked at least sixteen.

Gran smiled. "Okay, Ben, you're so eager to do it. I'll let you try being in charge of the money. But you've got to wear my fanny pack. It's the safest place for it."

There was no way Ben could see himself traipsing around like a geeky kid with a black pouch flapping over his stomach. He pulled his wallet out of his front pocket. "Our money will be totally safe here." He opened the wallet, folded the money Uncle Bob had given him and tucked it into a smaller pocket. He held open the main compartment. "See, lots of room for that wad of yours!"

Gran had her fingers on the zipper of her pack. "I'd worry you'd be pick-pocketed, Ben."

"Never! My wallet is a tight fit in the front pocket of my jeans."

Reluctantly, Gran handed Ben the rupee bills. They were

in a pile as thick as a paperback book. Ben packed them into his wallet, fastened the strap and stood up to stuff it in his pocket. He leaned his elbows on the table and grinned at Gran. It was a lot of money, but she'd see, he'd have no trouble taking care of it.

Gran smiled back. "First thing we need to do is take our malaria pills." She passed a cup of tea to Ben. "Then we go to find the house where Shanti's parents lived."

"Got the cash! I'm ready!" Ben said.

"Don't joke about it, Ben. I'm suddenly feeling nervous about going to Shanti's old house." Gran's hand shook as she put down her cup. "It's possible that Shanti's right here in Agra. I'm not sure I'm ready to meet her."

"Gimme a break, Gran. We've flown all the way from Canada, waited for two days at the registry office, travelled a whole day yesterday to get to Agra and now you get cold feet? Don't back out now!"

"You're right, Ben. I'm being silly."

Your words, not mine, Ben thought. Funny how one minute he'd be laughing hard with Gran and the next he'd be totally frustrated and irritated with her. At least he wouldn't have to watch her fumble with the money anymore.

A constant stream of cycle rickshaws came along the street, each cyclist hoping to be called over. A driver jumped down in front of them, pointing for them to use his rickshaw. He helped Gran get up into the seat and Ben got in beside her.

Gran took the address from her fanny pack. "We need to go to 187B Station Cross Road."

"Memsahib, I will take you there directly and safely," said their driver, springing onto his bike. "Though it will not be possible from here to be seeing the Taj Mahal, please do be enjoying the sights of Agra."

He cycled at a leisurely pace along streets full of shops and crowded with people. He carried on a conversation by turning around in his seat, his legs pedalling steadily. He told them his name was Nabir. "I am the proud father of four sons and one daughter who live with my wife far away in my home town."

"You don't live with them? You live here in Agra?"

"Yes and yes-no. For most of the year I live right here in my rickshaw."

It did look as though Nabir had all his worldly goods with him. Cloth bags and boxes were piled along the sides of the rickshaw, and there seemed to be more stored under the seat.

"My family live over one hundred kilometres to the east, and I visit them every year."

"You mean you only see your wife and children once a year?" Gran asked.

"Yes, but I am sending money to them every week. That is why I work hard."

Ben thought that even if you only saw your father once a year, at least you'd know he was coming back. Those kids were luckier than he was. He'd never see his dad again.

Nabir turned onto a street with a tidy row of houses and stopped at 187B. Gran and Ben looked at each other. This could be it. In one minute they could be seeing Shanti. A very wrinkled woman opened the door. Gran said, "We're looking for someone. Do you speak English?"

The woman shook her head and backed away, leaving the door slightly open. After a short wait, a young man appeared.

"I speak English," he said. "At least a little. How can I help you?"

Gran explained that the central registry office had given them this address for the Mukherjee family. The young man told them to wait while he asked his grandmother, who spoke only Hindi. He came back to say that his grandmother had lived in this house for thirty years and the residents before her were not called by that name. She thought older neighbours next door may have known the family. He would take them there.

The large house with an overgrown garden had an iridescent red and green parrot screeching at the world from its perch by the front door. Gran and Ben were introduced to the elderly couple who lived in the house.

The old man invited them to sit on the sofa and introduced himself as Mr. Sandhu. His wife was blind, he said, but her hearing was still good. They both listened carefully as Gran told her story.

"Indeed, we do know of them," said Mr. Sandhu, as his wife nodded. "In fact they were our friends many years ago."

Ben nudged Gran. At last. Gran had a smile on her face and sat forward on her seat. "How wonderful!"

"They were a lovely family," Mrs. Sandhu said in a frail voice. "We used to watch the young boy and girl playing in the garden."

"Was the girl called Shanti?" Ben asked.

"She could have been," said Mr. Sandhu.

"Yes, Shanti was her name," said Mrs. Sandhu, smiling. "She wore her hair in long braids. She was a serious girl, always reading."

Gran clapped her hands together. "That's Shanti for sure!"

"What happened to them?" Ben asked.

"The boy left to attend medical school."

"And Shanti?" said Ben. This was getting exciting.

"When she turned ten her parents sent her to a good girls' school, on the coast, I believe," said Mrs. Sandhu.

"Yes, I know about the school. I don't think it's there now," Gran said.

Ben wondered if it was time to let the cat out of the bag about trying to track Shanti down through the school site, but Gran had turned to the Sandhus to ask a question. "What about her parents? Are they still living?"

"They retired to Varanasi, east of here, to run a guest house. As far as I know, they are still there. Many tourists travel to Varanasi to bathe in the Ganges River, so owning a guest house there would provide a good income," Mr. Sandhu said.

"What was the name of the guest house?" Ben asked.

Mr. Sandhu shook his head. "Sadly, I am not able to re-member. You see, we lost touch completely."

"All this was many years ago. My husband and I are close to ninety," said Mrs. Sandhu.

Ben could see that Gran looked pale.

"Oh, to be so close," Gran said as she thanked the Sand-hus. She and Ben turned down the pathway of the garden and waved goodbye to the elderly couple as they reached the gate.

"Just a minute," called Mrs. Sandhu. "I've remembered that the guest house had the name Vishnu in it. Vishnu, yes . . . I'm sorry I can't remember more."

"Great!" Ben said. "That's a big help. We'll find it."

"There's an overnight train to Varanasi," called Mr. Sand-hu. "It leaves at ten in the evening and you arrive at five in the morning. Be sure to get an air-conditioned sleeper."

Mrs. Sandhu added, "Varanasi is India's most sacred city. Since your train arrives early, you must try to visit the river at sunrise. Then you must find a guest house with the name Vishnu."

Gran and Ben waved goodbye and started down the street. Suddenly Gran came to a halt. Her eyes scanned up and down the street as though she needed to memorize it. "I'm standing here knowing that Shanti walked on this street fifty years ago. I've got goose bumps all over my arms."

How a person could have goose bumps in such hot wea-ther was beyond Ben, but he knew what Gran meant. They hadn't found Shanti yet, but they seemed to be getting closer. He felt his pocket to make sure the wallet was there.

Curled up on the plastic seat of his rickshaw, Nabir dozed in the shade. Pleased at their news, he grinned at them, then jumped on his seat and began the long cycle back to the town centre.

Ben punched the air with his fist. "This is a hot lead, Gran. We'll take that train to Varanasi tonight. It won't be hard to find a guest house called Vishnu and I'll bet Shanti's parents are still there."

'You're more optimistic than I am, Ben. They'd be so old." Gran seemed to be afraid to count on anything. She sighed and squared her shoulders. "Now I think we should see the Taj Mahal. Maybe we should check out of the Hotel Rama first."

Going up the hotel steps, Ben said, "It's just too bad we won't have their deluxe service for another day!"

Gran gave a weak little laugh.

The desk clerk assured them he had a secure room behind the reception desk for their luggage. "Put your passports and visas in the packs. They will be safer here than in the crowds at the Taj Mahal. You will see," he said. He put the backpacks in the dark room and made a show of locking the door. "No need for a baggage ticket. I myself will be at the desk all day."

"Makes me a bit nervous leaving everything here," Gran said on their way out.

Ben made a face. "Never fear. Nothing can go wrong with Mr. Fix-it on the team."

This time he made Gran laugh out loud.

Nabir was waiting and gave them a ride to the entrance of the Taj Mahal.

Ben pulled out four hundred rupees for a tip and lifted his eyebrows in a question at Gran. She nodded and Ben handed the money to Nabir. "Maybe you can visit your family a few months early this year."

Without counting the bills, Nabir tucked them into an invisible pocket in his worn dhoti. "My thanks, and now I see that you will be having good fortune as the queue for the Taj is not so long." Ben wondered what he meant. The line-up was more than twice as long as a soccer field.

"What's so great about this Taj Mahal anyway?" he asked Gran, as they took their place at the end of the line.

"It's said to be the most beautiful building in the world, and it's special for me because Shanti talked about it."

After a long hot wait they reached the front of the line and the ticket booth. Ben purchased the entrance tickets and they went through a dim passageway, where a crowd of men waited to be hired as guides.

A man's voice beside them said, "Welcome, memsahib, and also to you, sir, with the fine Canadian hat. Please let me be your guide to this great testament to love we call the Taj Mahal."

"It's all right. We'll see it by ourselves," Gran said, turning away.

The guide followed behind and continued talking. "You must know that it was built by Emperor Shah Jehan as a burial spot for his beloved wife, who died giving birth to their fourteenth child."

Gran said, "I think we'd rather see it alone."

"Memsahib," the eager man answered. "I am able to point out the features of the Taj and also to instruct your son in the locations for the best photographs. He has a fine camera I see." The man had a big smile and the largest ears Ben had ever seen.

"I'm sure your services would cost a lot of money," Gran snapped.

"At the end of our time together, you may pay me whatever you think I'm worth," said the guide. "I have a university degree in history, so you may ask me any questions."

"Sounds like a good idea," Ben said. This guy seemed honest and he could use some help getting the best shots. If the man thought he was Gran's son, it didn't matter.

"We can manage, thank you," Gran said, dismissing the guide, who shrugged and turned away.

"I think we should have hired him," Ben said. "He's just trying to earn a living."

"People like that are after money from tourists, Ben. You and I can see everything on our own." She stopped by the archway. "Before we go in could you please buy some bottled water at the kiosk?"

The clerk placed the two bottles on the counter and Ben reached for his wallet. The pocket where he kept it was empty. So was the other pocket. Quickly, he searched his back pockets, even though he never put his wallet there. It was impossible, but the wallet was gone. Along with all Gran's money and his own too, it had vanished. Ben's face felt sweaty, and his scalp prickled. He always put the wallet back in his pocket. Somehow he must have dropped it. Or left it on the counter at the ticket booth. Yes, it was probably there.

Ben saw that his grandmother had her nose buried in a rack of postcards. Avoiding her, he made his way through the crowd to the ticket booth. "Sorry, sorry," he exclaimed, pushing past people waiting in line who'd probably see him as a rude North American tourist. Ben blurted, "I think I left my wallet here when I bought our tickets."

The cashier shook his head.

"It's blue," Ben said, gesturing with his hands. "This size." The cashier peered casually around the counter in front of him, shook his head again and turned to the next person in line.

It had to be somewhere. Ben scoured the floor around the ticket office; he got down on his knees and searched behind the booth, putting his fingers into the dark corners on the floor. He scrambled up and raced through the passageway, desperately looking everywhere. There was no wallet. He heard Gran calling him and made his way through the guides, all the time scanning the floor for a blue wallet.

"Where'd you disappear to?" Gran asked.

"Just trying to find water," Ben lied. "The kiosk didn't have any." Amazing how easy it was to lie. He realized he'd do anything to avoid telling Gran he'd lost their money. Lost it the same day she'd given it to him.

Gran didn't question his explanation and began heading through the archway into the garden leading to the Taj. Ben followed her along a path beside two reflecting pools. He barely noticed the massive white dome framed with four slender towers ahead of them. His mind was reeling. Where was his wallet?

Ben looked over at Gran and saw tears rolling down her cheeks. What was it now? His grandmother wiped her eyes with the back of her hand. "It's like a giant pearl floating in space. I've never seen anything so beautiful. I think of Shanti standing right here and remember all over again how much I want to see her." Gran covered her face with her hands and began to sob.

Ben stood beside her, mortified at his grandmother's blubbering noises. He patted her arm. If she cried like this over a building, she'd be uncontrollable when she found out all their money was lost.

Across the lawn a worker led a grey bullock pulling a lawn-mower. Ben tried to distract his grandmother. "Look at that. A new way to mow the grass, Gran!"

His grandmother lifted her head, wiping her nose and sniffling like a kid.

Ben needed time, and he had an idea. "Let me see your guidebook, Gran."

He'd try reading to her to give himself time to think. Ben sat down on a marble bench and motioned her to sit beside him. He began reading. "Says here, it took twenty-one years and twenty thousand workers to complete the building. And after the work was finished, the Shah cut off the hands of his workmen!"

"Why would he do that?"

"Apparently he wanted to make sure no other building in the Mogul empire could ever be as beautiful as this one, because no other love could match his love for his wife."

One glance told him she was starting to cry again.

Ben had a flash that maybe, just maybe, this place had a Lost and Found and his wallet had been turned in. Now he was desperate to get back to the entrance. "We should leave," Ben said, grabbing his grandmother's arm in an attempt to pull her off the bench.

"Ben! We just got here. I want to sit and enjoy this place." She pushed his arm away. "What's the matter with you anyway?"

He'd have to lie again. "Gran, I . . . you know. I've got bad stomach cramps. I think it's something I ate. I have to get to the toilet. Right away." He clutched his stomach, turned and rushed back through the passageway.

If he was lucky and his wallet was at the Lost and Found, Gran would never need to know he'd lost the money. The crowd scattered on either side as he rushed down the middle. So many people, so many of them poor — it would be a miracle if anyone had turned his wallet in.

Once again, Ben pushed his way to the front of the line at the ticket booth. A new cashier was selling tickets at the counter. He frowned as Ben explained. The man barely looked at him. "We have no Lost and Found. Sorry."

Again Ben hunted in every corner of the entrance and into the passage. He shoved his way through the guides, looking around the floor, up and over all the sandals, the slippers, the clogs, the loafers, the sneakers, big and little, until he found himself back in the sunny courtyard in front of the Taj.

Gran was still sitting on the bench and had stopped crying. She saw his face. "You look terrible, Ben."

"I'm all right," he said.

"Are you sure?"

"Yep, I'm just going to wander around and take some pictures." He had no idea what to do next. With his heart thumping, he quickly shot pictures of the Taj. Then he got a photograph of the bullock mowing the lawn. Another of two little children trailing behind their mother. Another one of the bullock.

"Do you want to go, Ben?" Gran said as she came up behind him.

"I'm not in a hurry now," Ben said. Why couldn't he just lie down and bury his head in the grass and never have to explain anything to anyone?

"I don't like the way you look. Come on, let's go back to the hotel."

On the way out, Gran stopped at the postcard rack. "These cards have the story about the Taj on the back. I'll pick some out and you can pay for them."

Ben froze. "I've got good pictures, Gran. You don't need postcards."

"But I can mail these, Ben. I'd like to send cards back to Canada."

He couldn't put if off any longer. He'd have to tell her. Ben heard himself mumble. "I can't pay for them."

"What did you say?"

"I don't have the money, Gran."

"What?"

"I don't have the money. I lost my wallet."

Gran's voice seemed very loud. "You're telling me you've been robbed?"

"I don't know. I think I might have dropped the wallet. They don't have a Lost and Found here. I've searched everywhere."

Gran threw her hands in the air, shook them and let them drop. "I knew it. You've been pick-pocketed. I was stupid to let you keep all our money in that wallet!" She was yelling now.

"Calm down, Gran."

Frantically she began to sweep her eyes around the entranceway. "I think I know who did it. That man who was pestering us to hire him as our guide. He got a little too close. He took it!"

Then, at exactly the same moment, both Gran and Ben saw the man Gran had been talking about come toward them. Ben recognized the man's big ears — and his own blue wallet in the man's outstretched hand.

"I believe this belongs to you?" the guide said.

"It does! Where did you find it?" Ben said.

"It was turned in to the man at the water kiosk and I told him I thought I'd seen you with it as you came in from the ticket booth. I remembered your Canada hat." With an easy smile, he handed the wallet to Ben. "Please check inside. I think you will find the money there, but please count it."

Gran's face broke into a smile and she reached out to shake the guide's hand. "Thank you so much."

"You are most welcome, indeed, memsahib. I do hope your son got some good photographs."

"She's my grandmother," Ben said.

"I would never have guessed. The memsahib looks so young."

Gran was beaming at him. "We'd like to give you a reward."

"No, no, memsahib. Most happy to be of service." The guide made the *namaste* gesture and turned to join the other guides.

Gran said, "I feel so guilty thinking that nice man had robbed you."

"Just goes to show, most people are honest."

"You are one lucky boy, Ben."

"I know I'm lucky. It was scary." Ben started to put the wallet in his pocket. "I don't know how I lost it. I always put it back in my pocket. I'll be extra careful with the money from now on, Gran. It will never happen again, I promise."

Gran stopped in her tracks. "Benjamin, it will never happen again because if you want to handle the money, you'll be wearing my fanny pack."

Ben shook his head. "I can't do it. I'd feel too lame."

Gran's jaw was set. "Then give the money back to me." She opened the zipper. "It will be safe in my pack, even though you think it's funny."

For a millisecond, Ben thought maybe he *could* wear the fanny pack. After all, nobody knew him in India. Then he realized there was no way; he'd rather be seen wearing his grandmother's skirt than the belly pouch. He took out the bills and handed them to his grandmother. Not looking at her, he stomped on ahead.

"Sorry, but that's the way it has to be, Ben." Gran said, rushing along behind him. "We should hurry. The train leaves at ten, and we've got to collect our backpacks at the hotel."

Ben sat on the rickshaw as far apart from his grandmother as he could. It had been such a scare losing the wallet. His legs were still shaky. He felt stupid and embarrassed, but Gran should understand that anyone could lose a wallet once in their life. Now she'd taken away his chance to show it would never happen again.

Ben crossed his arms over his chest and turned his head away from his grandmother. He was first up the steps of the Hotel Rama. It was almost eight.

The clerk at the reception desk was a man they'd never seen before.

"Our backpacks are locked in that room behind the desk," Ben said.

The clerk disappeared and returned with a small black overnight bag. "This is the only thing in our storeroom," he said, shaking his head.

"I know our two backpacks are there. We saw the clerk put them in the room," Ben said. "Where is the afternoon clerk?"

"He went home early with a bad ache," said the new clerk.

"We need our packs. We have to get to the train station tonight," Gran almost shouted. "Please get the manager."

"No manager on night duty, madam," the clerk said firmly.

Ben began to search the lobby. He opened one door to a bathroom and another that led to a set of stairs. This was crazy. How could two backpacks disappear?

Gran paced back and forth in front of the desk. "Every single thing we own is in those bags. Our passports. Our visas. Our airline tickets."

"I wonder if they could be in our room?" Ben said.

"Most certainly I do not think so," said the clerk, defiantly. "You are being checked out of the hotel and your room will have been cleaned."

"Why not let me look in the room?" Ben asked.

"No, sir, we cannot do that. You see, you are being checked out. But I will call our porter. He will look for us."

He ran the bell on his desk twice. They waited. Gran perched on a dirty chair in the lobby. She was taking deep breaths. Ben stalked back and forth in a steady path in the lobby. It was now twenty minutes past eight.

"Do not worry," said the desk clerk. "The train station is a short walk from here."

After ten minutes, their old friend, Mr. Fix-it, shuffled into the lobby.

"Oh, no," Gran said. "I can't believe it." Her face was scarlet. Ben wondered if that's how a person looked when they were about to have a heart attack.

"Let him try to find it, Gran," Ben said.

It was another long wait before Mr. Fix-it came down the stairs, making a big show of carrying the two backpacks. "This afternoon I am seeing the bags, and I am having them returned to your room."

Gran glared at the man. Mr. Fix-it dropped the two packs and stretched out his hand for a tip. "You are being most welcome."

"The man is beyond belief," Gran muttered, picking up her backpack and heading for the door. Ben followed and when they were outside, burst out laughing. "That guy actually expected us to give him a fat tip!"

Gran trotted along, muttering about the "stupid old fool in the stupid Hotel Rama."

"Chill, Gran. It wasn't a hotel, remember? It was an experience."

"Never to be repeated, I hope," she said.

"We got our bags. Lighten up."

Inside the huge train station there was a line for tickets to Varanasi. Ben told Gran he'd be in the internet office at the other side of the station.

She nodded. "I'll wait in the line. Watch your wallet."

At one end of the terminal whole families camped in small groups along the walls. Women were crouched over cooking pots on Primus stoves; children wrapped in shawls sat cross-legged around the warmth of the flame. Other children, covered with rough blankets, stretched out asleep on the bare concrete floor. A grey-haired grandmother, her eyes closed, sat with her back to the wall, cradling a baby in a sling next to her thin body. Hot steam curling up from the cooking pots carried the smell of curry and spices into the homey space around each family.

The internet office at the end of the station was a hot, narrow room with three ancient computers along a counter. The man in charge told Ben it would cost two hundred rupees for fifteen minutes. It was outrageous, but he paid. First he'd email home.

> Dear Mum and Lauren
>
> I accidentally lost our money, but we got it back. Now Gran refuses 2 let me take care of it unless I wear her stupid fanny pack. She has 2 have her way about everything and it's driving me kra-zee. We're leaving for Varanasi on the train.
>
> Ben

Next the school site. Ben's heart was beating hard as he keyed it in. It seemed to take a long time, and he blinked in disbelief when he found there was no response. Mrs. Rau had said that former students regularly checked their school sites for messages, but maybe it would take another day or two for a former student to spot the request. What was it Gandhi had said? Patience and persistence. He had to work on that.

When Ben returned to the ticket stall, Gran had two tickets in her hand: air-conditioned second class tickets in Car 37. They headed out along the platform, past railcars where people would be sitting up on wooden seats all night. At the very end of the train they found Car 37. They climbed the steps into a steamy windowless compartment where wooden bunk beds lined the sides of a narrow passage. Their beds were across from an older man on the lower bunk and a young couple sharing the upper bunk. There was a ladder to their top bunk and heavy blue curtains provided privacy from travellers across the aisle.

Gran checked out the ladder. "You mind taking the top bunk, Ben?"

"Whatever you say," Ben said.

The man showed them how to lock their backpacks to the chain that ran from the floor to the ceiling to keep them from being stolen, but Gran shook her head. "We nearly lost everything we owned at an awful hotel. I'll sleep better with my backpack right beside me."

The couple on the top bunk across from Ben had settled

down for the night; he could hear soft whispers and rustling noises that made him think *they* weren't finding it too crowded.

"Don't we get a sheet or a blanket?" Ben asked.

The man said, "Don't worry, you won't need anything. It will get so hot up there you'll bake like tandoori chicken."

Gran leaned out of her bunk and pointed at the ceiling. "Don't tell me that's our air-conditioning?"

Ben stared at a dilapidated wooden fan with two broken blades. It was moving in a slow jerking circle precariously close to his bunk. He decided not to undress and made a pillow out of his rolled up jacket. He shoved his pack under his feet and tried to settle his body on the hard wood.

He lay awake wincing at the erratic motion of the ceiling fan. Only when the blades slid with a jolt toward him did he feel the smallest movement of air, and with it, the heavy smell of too many bodies in too small a space.

The train started with a bump, then rocked and swayed along the track as Ben closed his eyes. No matter how far away you were or what kind of a strange place you were in, you carried your sadness with you. Ben remembered that Dad had promised him a train trip across Canada. "You'll love it," he said. "The prairies are something to see. I'll take you to the place where I grew up. It was a two-grain-elevator town." Well, that would never happen. Ben could feel himself slide down into sleep.

He was sitting with Dad in the train's restaurant car. They were at a table with a white cloth and the waiter had just served bacon and eggs on silver plates. Out the window Ben saw a solid blue sky and long golden prairie fields. Dad was pointing to two red grain elevators in the distance. "Let me tell you what it was like growing up in a small town like that . . ."

Suddenly the train came to a rasping halt and Ben heard voices from outside. His watch said 2:20 a.m.

"You asleep, Ben?" Gran whispered.

"I was in the middle of a dream."

"Sorry if I woke you."

"It's okay. It was only a dumb dream."

"Ben, you didn't have stomach cramps at the Taj, did you?"

"No."

"I'm glad."

"It's so hot I'm being cremated up here."

"It's going to be a long night."

The train bolted to a start again. It had been a horrible day. The only thing that would make this trip worthwhile would be if he could surprise Gran by finding Shanti. And for that he needed one person out there who knew her to check in with the school website. Just one person.

Day Six

"VARANASI! VARANASI!"

Where was he? Ben peered into the dark. The muggy air drifting from the fitful fan reminded him that he was in the top bunk on a train in the middle of India. It was five in the morning and the difficult night's journey was over.

Ben's shoulders ached and he had a cramp in one foot as he and Gran joined the other half-awake passengers disembarking from the train.

"I'm sore in every part of my old bod," Gran said, as she trudged stiffly beside him to the station exit. "Let's find a taxi."

"It's pitch dark out here," Ben said, "but look at the line of taxis." The first driver nodded when Gran asked for a guest house called Vishnu. They left the station and turned onto a main road with the car's single headlight guiding them. The taxi stopped in front of a small hotel with a sign: VISHNU LODGE.

"Maybe we're getting lucky," Ben said. He could see Gran's lips pinched with nervousness.

Their backpacks seemed heavier this morning as they came into the lobby and went up to a desk clerk who was sound asleep with his head down on the desk.

"Sorry to wake you. Good morning," Gran said.

The clerk's head jerked up.

"We'd like a room with two beds please," Gran said. "And we'd also like to know the name of the owners of the lodge."

"Most certainly I have a room available for you," the clerk said in a groggy voice. "The new owner, memsahib, is Mr. Gupta. He has just recently purchased the establishment. Would you like to talk to him?"

Gran's voice was tight. "I guess we'll need information about the previous owners."

"Mr. Gupta will help you. He is, of course, sleeping in his room upstairs, but I will give him your message when he wakes."

As Gran signed the register, Ben tried to reassure her. "The owner probably bought the lodge from Shanti's parents. I bet they're still in Varanasi."

The clerk handed Gran the room key. "May I suggest,

since you are so clearly awake, that now would be an excellent time to visit our holy Ganges River. The Ganga, as we call it, is an unforgettable sight at dawn."

The clerk carried their bags upstairs and brought two cups of hot chai to the room. From the window he pointed to a narrow lane across from the hotel that would take them to something he called the ghats at the river.

"Let's go," Ben said, rushing to drink the spicy sweet tea. "We can't go back to bed, and by the time we get back from the river, the owner will be up."

Gran's hair was unbrushed and she still looked sleepy, but she agreed. She finished her chai while Ben found his camera in his backpack.

They felt their way down the outside steps of their hotel and crossed the dark street to the lane. More men and women joined them until they were part of a crowd, some people limping or using crutches. All were silent in the early morning darkness.

At one corner a beggar woman carrying a baby wrapped in rags grabbed at Gran's arm. Gran jerked back, stepping onto the tail of a pale mongrel dog that had been scrounging for garbage at the side of the lane. The cur snarled, moved closer and bared its teeth. Gran backed away. Without thinking, Ben stepped between his grandmother and the dog, then took Gran's arm and guided her ahead.

"Thanks for protecting me, Ben," Gran said. "That dog was mean enough to take a chunk out of my leg."

"No problem," Ben said. It felt good to be watching out for his grandmother.

The lanes opened onto a large square, and in the dim light Gran and Ben had their first sight of the wide Ganga.

Gran said, "Those must be what the hotel clerk called the ghats." She pointed to stone steps leading into the water.

At the top of the ghats, they were swarmed by eager boatmen. Like chickens scurrying to peck at the tourists, the men called: "Look this way." "See the sights, memsahib." "Come with me! Five hundred rupees for one hour." "Here is the best safe boat. Very cheap too."

They found themselves being herded down the steps by a small man with a bare chest and a dhoti twisted between his thin legs. It was as though he'd done the choosing and swept them up before they'd had a chance to think about it. The man's dark eyes gleamed at them over a sharp nose. "You will be calling me Anoop," he said. "I am your best guide here and I will have answers to all your questions." He acted as if they were lucky he'd chosen them.

Anoop helped them board his open rowboat, where a man and a woman were already seated, clutching at the sides of the rocking vessel. Gran and Ben sat down on the seat across from them; then Anoop hopped in and took up the oars, guiding the boat out into the swiftly flowing river.

"Seems we have fellow Canadians here," said the woman. She nodded at Ben's baseball cap and introduced herself as Martha and her husband as Geoffrey Bonder, from Calgary.

Martha had long straight hair and wore a flowered skirt with leather sandals. Geoffrey had a huge camera around his neck and an Adam's apple that bounced like a yo-yo over the collar of his brown shirt. He was wearing the same awful hat as Gran, along with an ugly fishing vest completely covered in pockets.

"I see you're a fan of Tilley stuff, too," he said, laughing and pointing to Gran's hat. "This vest is a Tilley *and* so's my underwear! Great stuff — dries in an hour."

Please let this not be true, Ben thought. Two Tilley freaks in one boat. If the water hadn't been covered with yellow scum he might have jumped overboard.

"I'm Norah Leeson and this is my grandson Ben," Gran said. "Aren't we all a long way from Canada."

Anoop pointed to the east and signalled his passengers to watch across the river. Ben had seen a few great sunrises camping with Dad, but none were a match for this. Rising above the horizon was the largest crimson sun he'd ever seen. Beside them, other boats bobbed in the murky water, their passengers under a collective trance at the magnificence of the morning, their faces bathed in the reflected glow of the red ball of the enormous sun. To complete the picture, the sound of clanging temple bells drifted across from the shore. Ben felt as though he were in the middle of a movie set.

A smaller boat approached their side and a sari-clad woman held up a coconut shell with a small lit candle inside. A wooden shelf stretched across her boat; on it sat more shells, each containing a glowing candle.

Anoop explained, "You must have a candle to float on the river. They will be keeping company with the ashes of the departed for their journey to the next world."

Gran handed Ben coins to pay for the candles, while Geoffrey, who was like a walking filing cabinet, scrabbled through one vest pocket after another trying to find his money. One by one, Anoop's passengers leaned over the side of the boat to put their shells in the water.

Ben watched his own small flame drift away. Was his father, too, one of the departed on a journey to the next world? Was there a next world? If he could understand what happened after someone died, maybe he'd find a way to stop feeling so angry. His shell bobbed farther and farther away to join the floating jetsam of banana peels, blobs of plastic and orange flowers.

As the sky lightened, their boat continued south along the rows of ghats that made an endlessly shifting scene before them. Against a backdrop of temple spires, hundreds of people had crowded onto the steps. Men and women, still fully dressed in their clothes, waded into the rosy-hued river to soap and wash themselves, the women's saris billowing around them as they submerged to rinse their hair in the filthy water. In one place, a man had taken his cow to the river to be scrubbed. Beside the cow, whose body was lathered in soap, a young mother and her two children were splashing and playing.

Anoop explained, "Since the seventh century bathing is being a Hindu morning ritual in Varanasi."

Ben found it impossible to believe that he was tossing around in a small boat on a holy river thousands of miles away from home. This was real life, more amazing than any computer game ever invented.

On the top steps, lean yogis had taken up their positions, twisting their legs like pretzels around their necks. Other men, as unmoving as statues, sat with their feet folded into the lotus position, their palms together in a *namaste* prayer.

"They are doing *pujas*," said the boatman.

"What are they?" Ben asked.

"*Pujas* are our prayers, and just as Hindus must be bathing every day at sunrise, so they must be saying their *pujas*."

Ben peered across the water at a large object floating toward them. He pointed. "Over there, what's that?"

As the thing floated nearer, Ben saw it was the bloated black body of a cow. With its legs stiffly in the air, the body bounced up and down, coming closer and closer to their boat. Ben stared in horror. Good thing Lauren wasn't there. She'd be totally freaked out.

"Ugh! Horrible," Gran said. Geoffrey and Martha groaned and turned their heads away, but Ben found himself unable to stop looking. As he watched, the waves tossed the cow's body over to his side of their small boat. The nearer it came the more Ben could see. The poor animal's face was swollen grey, its mouth set in a grimace, the cloudy eyes popped out like milky marbles. The cow's stomach was distended like a pregnant hippo's, and as it came nearer, the stench of rotting flesh made Ben pinch his nose shut.

"It's going to hit the boat!" Martha screamed.

"Its stomach will burst and send pus all over us," Geoffrey said, hunching his shoulders and pulling his hat over his face. Martha screamed again, trying to pull part of her flowered skirt over her head, which showed her hairy legs.

Anoop was straining at the oars as fast as he could, but the dead cow had bumped against the boat. Ben reached for a metal pole at his feet. One end of the pole was sharp but luckily the other was blunt. He pushed the blunt end into the cow's tough hide and pushed with all his strength. Gradually, the cow was caught by the current and swept out to the middle of the river.

Geoffrey was ashen and his Adam's apple was vibrating. "Good grief, Ben, we could have had that cow's innards all over us. You've got a quick head on you not to poke with the sharp end."

"Good work, Ben," said Gran.

"Thank you for assisting, young man," said Anoop.

Ben was concentrating on getting his heart beat back to normal.

"What's a dead cow doing in the water anyway?" Martha said, smoothing her skirt over her knees.

Anoop explained that it was a usual practice for a cow's body to be tossed in the river. "As you must be knowing, our cows are holy. When they are dying, it is always of natural causes and they are never burned. Our beloved Ganga is taking them peacefully to the next life."

Ben had missed his chance to take a picture, and by now,

the cow was too far away to look like anything more than a tree stump floating in the river. Just as well. Lauren and his mum would not want to see it. It had really been an amazing sight, though, and he felt proud of himself for not freaking out when the body had come so close.

As the morning advanced, more and more boats floated around them. People shouted to each other across the ghats, sounds of chanting drifted from the temples, dogs barked, and from the streets farther away came the honking of horns.

"Now we will return past the burning ghats," Anoop said.

"Martha and I have read in our guidebook about the burnings," Geoffrey said. He was still nervous, patting his pockets and adjusting his hat.

Anoop turned the boat around, and it bounced precariously upriver past piles of wood stacked on the river bank.

Anoop pointed to a wooden platform where a body lay wrapped in white cloth. "This is the funeral pyre. You will see the grieving relatives." A family stood beside a platform watching as a robed priest poured yellow liquid over the body, and then gestured for the family to stand back.

The priest used a torch to light the fire, which became a signal for the keening wails of the female relatives to begin. Like the calls of high birds, the sounds carried across the water to their boat. Trailing behind came the smell of the blaze as the wrappings around the body caught fire. It was not the clean smell of a campfire, but the heavy stench of burning rags; and then another smell, sharp and sickening.

Burning hair. Ben remembered his sister reaching over her birthday candles, the few strands of her hair, flaring only briefly, but filling the room with alarm.

Suddenly the flames burst into a lashing red and for an instant Ben saw the clear outline of the body. He saw the head of the corpse, the arms folded across the chest and the outstretched legs. He heard the crackle of burning flesh. Other sounds came into Ben's head. *The heavy thud, thud at the graveside as they took turns shovelling dirt on his father's coffin. The March wind shaking the branches of the tall cedars that lined the edge of the burial ground. His mother and grandmother and Lauren crying.*

He had not cried once. He remembered the heaviness of the shovel in his hands, how dirt had stuck to the handle and the dusty smell that stayed on his hands all that day.

He'd never thought of asking why his father wasn't cremated. In some ways, burning was simpler. You weren't forced to think about the body of a person you loved rotting slowly in the grave.

Ben checked his grandmother and saw the grim set of her mouth as she watched the burning pyre. No one spoke. When he turned back, the outline of the corpse was lost in the fire, which now sent long orange fingers into the sky, like a Halloween bonfire. Only it wasn't Halloween. In front of their eyes, a body with skin and bones, arms and legs was being transformed into ashes.

Ben reached to take his camera from around his neck, but before he could open the case, Anoop put his arm out to stop him. "Respectfully sir, you must be putting your camera away. To Hindus it shows dishonour to photograph the dead. Our boat could be rammed and we would be seriously harmed."

Anoop was funny the way he talked, but it wouldn't be funny to end up in this water. Ben looked up and saw four large grey birds winding in low circles over the river bank. He heard Martha shriek, "Vultures!"

"Yes," said Anoop. "The vultures have much work here in Varanasi."

Gran and the others turned their eyes away, but Ben watched the birds as they circled endlessly around the pyres. Ugly birds, he thought, caught up in a gruesome death cycle.

A short distance downriver, two men and two young boys carrying a brass pan started to wade into the water. "Watch as they are scattering the ashes of their loved one for the journey to the afterlife," Anoop said.

The boys threw handful after handful of ashes onto the water, then ducked their heads under, lifting their faces up into the floating ashes.

"They are having the bath of purification," Anoop explained.

What would it be like to be a Hindu boy and feel your own father's ashes in your eyes and your mouth? Ben shuddered. He couldn't do it.

"I've seen enough, Anoop," Gran said. "Is anyone else ready to go back?"

Ben had seen enough too. Seen enough, and remembered enough.

Anoop bowed in thanks when Gran and Geoffrey Bonder each gave him a tip and they all watched as he hurried across the ghats in search of new passengers.

Now the large square was a crowded scene full of more amazing sights. Barbers stood behind stools as they cut men's hair and shaved their faces. Vendors with boom boxes blaring from their stalls sold coloured powders as cures for every illness. At long tables, women offered hot breakfasts of steaming chapatis and fried triangles of parathas.

"Will you look at that!" Martha pointed to a man who was lighting the tops of long thin candles and inserting them into his customer's ears.

Geoffrey said, "I've read about them. They're ear cleaners, if you can believe it."

In the middle of the chaotic square, tawny-coloured cows pushed freely through the crowds. In one corner a man, so thin that his stomach had sunk almost to his backbone, lay on a bed of nails. His eyes were closed but his palm was outstretched, waiting for donations. A dwarf standing beside him also had his doll-like hand out, and farther along another man balanced on one leg. A rough sign in English said he hadn't rested on a bed for twenty years.

"He wants us to give him money because he's been standing on one leg for twenty years!" Martha said. "It's unbelievable."

Ben, who was behind Martha, saw that her long skirt was caught up between her legs. Gross. He hurried on ahead.

Geoffrey and Martha were also staying at the Vishnu Lodge, and Gran decided they'd have breakfast together. As they turned into an alley, four men came down the narrow passageway toward them. Above their heads they carried a bamboo stretcher; laid out on it was a small body wrapped in white cotton. The smell of musty cedar hung in the air as the men's raised arms brushed Ben's shoulder.

Ben realized with horror that he could have reached up and touched the dead body. This was the closest he'd been to a dead person since his father had died. And this body was so small you could tell it was a child. Here in Varanasi Ben found it impossible to pull the curtain down on his thoughts. He was in a city of death.

Farther along, a skinny pig rooted in garbage beside two black rats that fought over the scraps, their long tails flicking over the sow's feet. The smell was worse than the rotting egg sandwich Ben had left in a plastic bag in his locker for three weeks. Worse than five thousand rotting egg sandwiches. Gran and Martha kept their hands over their mouths.

The streets widened and they heard the sound of tinny bells coming from a courtyard. Around the corner, Ben saw a large stone temple, and outside it, an elephant in a dirt enclosure. The shocking thing was that the elephant was chained by one of its front legs to a stake in the ground. The elephant was small and probably young, though it was hard for Ben to know. As he watched, the sad creature lifted his plate-sized foot, straining to get free. Raising his trunk, the elephant began to bellow plaintively.

"That poor elephant!" Ben said. He went closer.

"Don't go in there," Geoffrey said. "I've read that only Hindus are allowed to enter temple grounds."

"It's terrible. That poor elephant can't move. He needs to get free," Ben said.

"Ben, come with us," Gran called.

Reluctantly, Ben followed the adults as they made their way to the Kwality Restaurant next to the guest house.

"Hope you two are taking your malaria pills," Martha said. "A friend of ours got a bad case of malaria down here. Forgot to take his pills. He was one sick man."

Geoffrey added, "Guess you heard the one about Indian hospitals not being so bad?"

"No, don't think we have," Gran said.

"It's a good one," Martha said, leaning toward her husband.

Geoffrey puffed himself up. "Well, it seems a man got sick in India and went to the door of an Indian hospital. He took one look inside and turned away. Cured."

Ben frowned and looked at his grandmother.

"Funny, eh." Geoffrey said. "Get it?"

"I don't," Ben said, turning toward Gran.

Gran explained. "It means the sick man took one look inside the hospital, and things were so terrible, he said he was cured so he wouldn't have to go inside."

Ben wasn't certain he understood, but he decided to let it go.

"Remember you heard it here," Geoffrey said, laughing with Martha.

"We'll be sure to remember," Gran said.

Ben bent his head to his breakfast while Gran told the Bonders how the search for Shanti had taken them from Delhi to Agra and now Varanasi. "As soon as we finish eating we're meeting the new owner to see if he knows anything about Shanti's parents."

They found Mr. Gupta at the reception desk. It turned out that he'd purchased the lodge from a young couple who'd moved to Calcutta. Mr. Gupta thought for a minute. "You know, there is another guest house called the Old Vishnu on the other side of town. I suggest you try there."

Ben wrote down the address. "We should go there now, Gran."

Gran answered. "Ben, I'm beat. After that sleepless night on the train I have to lie down awhile before we go anywhere."

Ben followed her, noticing how slowly she climbed the stairs. He went into the bathroom and washed his face in cold water. Gran was lying down when he came out.

What a morning. A bloated cow with its legs sticking up in the air. The smell of the body burning on the pyre. The little corpse being carried so close to him in the alley. But it was the elephant tied up beside the temple that kept returning to Ben's thoughts. "I'm not tired, Gran," he said. "I'd like to go back and find out about the elephant we saw."

"Forget that," Gran said, lifting her head from the bed. "There's no way I'm letting a boy your age wander around alone." Her head slipped back and she closed her eyes.

Ben went to the window and looked down at the labyrinth of narrow streets. It was not yet noon. He checked his grandmother. Her steady snores told him she had fallen asleep. How could anyone sleep with so many amazing things just a step away? He could see the dome of the temple and could almost hear the pitiful bellow of the chained elephant.

Ben opened the door and stepped out.

Still Day Six

IT WASN'T FAR TO the temple. Ben hurried through the gate and over to the enclosure that roped off the small elephant. The elephant grunted, short frustrated grunts, as it strained to be free of the chain around his foot. Ben stepped close. "Easy, easy."

The elephant's wrinkled skin was mottled with dirt from its struggles. It had no tusks and his grey ears were freckled right out to the ragged edges. Ben reached over to run his hand along the elephant's trunk. The trunk was warm and leathery, only about as thick as a mountain bike tire.

The elephant stopped pulling and turned its sad eyes to watch Ben. It was those eyes, Ben thought . . . There was something so ancient and knowing about them that made you feel an elephant really saw you. You were communicating with an animal who really knew who you were.

Ben picked up a handful of hay at the edge of the enclosure and held it out. The pink tip of the elephant's trunk curled around the straw and swung it into his mouth. Ben watched him chew.

"At least you're eating," Ben said. He gave the elephant more hay and stroked its trunk. It was a great feeling.

He took a photograph of the elephant, then scanned the courtyard to see if anyone seemed as if they were responsible for it. People were rushing in from the entrance talking among themselves, but no one cast a glance at the elephant. No one seemed to care that the poor thing was suffering.

Again, the elephant lifted his foot and strained at the chain. He could only move such a short distance that his struggles traced a circle in the dust around the post.

Maybe there was a caretaker nearer the temple. Ben joined the crowd heading up the wide stone steps, past a row of pillars onto the wide porch. People were taking off their sandals and handing them to an old man who seemed to be a shoe guard.

The man held out his hand for Ben's runners, and with a shock Ben saw that the man had shrivelled hollows instead of eyes.

Pouring through the temple door into a gloomy corridor, the crowd swept Ben along with them. No one noticed him and no one stopped him. The dirt under his bare feet was wet and slippery. He could be infected with some horrible foot disease.

The smoky smell of incense made Ben light-headed. The dark passageway twisted and narrowed; rough stone walls pressed in on either side. Ben could see only as far as the cotton shirt of the man ahead of him. Drums began to beat, and as he went farther, the beating became a louder, more insistent throbbing. The crush of people behind pressed him forward. It was impossible to turn back.

Gran had been right. He didn't belong here with the sickening smell, the pounding drums, the bodies hemming him in so that he had no choice but to go where they took him. Deep in an underground maze, he was being led closer to something or someone, he didn't know what.

At the next turn, the passageway opened onto an alcove lit by the flare of oil lamps against the damp walls. This must be the inner sanctuary, the home of the god who ruled this temple. Ben pushed his way to the front of the crowd. What he saw appalled him.

It must be Black Kali, the goddess of destruction. The goddess even Padam had been scared of, the one who demanded sacrifices. About three metres high, the statue sat on a platform draped in dark cloth. The black face had bulging white eyes and a protruding tongue dripping with what looked like blood. Kali's dark hair was tossed in all directions and her ten twisting arms held knives and swords, and in one, a bleeding head. A necklace of bony skulls circled her shoulders, and at her feet, visitors had placed bananas and coconuts. The throbbing of the drums was so loud that Ben's head spun; he felt he was smothering at the centre of the transported worshippers.

A bare-chested Brahmin priest appeared from behind the god. He carried a brass tray spread with burning coals and a container of red powder. A smell as strong and sickly as rotting fruit leapt up from the flames. The priest reached into the flames with his finger, then into the red powder and pressed a mark on the forehead of each worshipper. Ben tried to step back, but couldn't. He felt the priest's hot finger press between his eyes. At that very moment Kali's huge eyeballs turned on Ben, and her flailing arms reached out to draw him closer. He swayed, pitching toward the statue. Kali's hooked red fingernails stretched out to touch him.

Ben heard his breath become shallow, faster. It felt as though he were running, but he wasn't. This was what fear felt like. He was more scared than he'd ever been in his life. With all his strength, Ben backed through the crowd, turned and ran, fled as fast as he could, away from Kali's bulging eyes and red tongue and the reaching arms, away from the smells and the burning coals and, most of all, away from the incessant drumming.

Alone now in the dark corridor, Ben gasped for breath, stumbled and kept running. He struck a sharp corner, his feet slipped in the mud and he fell to his knees. Struggling to stand, Ben reached to the stone wall for support. His hand touched something moist and slimy, something horribly like a swollen slug. He snapped his hand back and stood up, trying to wipe the stickiness away on his pants. He could feel cold mud from the floor on his legs. Nothing he could do about that now. He had to get a grip on himself so he could find a way out.

What was he doing inside a temple? He wasn't a Hindu. He was just a kid. Why hadn't anyone stopped him? A stab of pure terror pierced Ben's stomach. He was alone in an endless black tunnel. Not one person knew where he was.

He strained to see ahead into the darkness. He had to find a way out. Was that a light? Another alcove? Or had he been running in a circle and come back to the terrifying Kali?

Ben took a few cautious steps until he was close enough to see light coming from a smaller sanctuary. He looked inside and saw a statue of Ganesh with a garland of yellow marigolds draped over the god's round belly. Here was the god Ben knew, the elephant god who listened to children.

Ben looked into the almost human eyes of the elephant. *Help me*, he pleaded silently . . . and then it happened. In the dim light, the elephant's stone trunk swayed, lifted and dipped, dipped away from the passage Ben had been following toward a dark narrow tunnel he hadn't noticed.

Ganesh's eyes: they were eyes you could trust. Against all reason, the stone trunk had moved to show him the way out. Yes, he could trust Ganesh. Ben turned in the direction of the pointing trunk to the dark opening. He began to run, faster and faster. Then, without warning, he burst out into bright sunshine and stepped onto grass.

His chest hurt. He strained to gulp the fresh air as he looked around. There were no crowds of people, no piles of shoes. Maybe he was at the back of the temple, and if he followed the temple wall, he might reach the front entrance. Steadying himself by pressing his hands against the stone, his bare feet pricked by the coarse grass, Ben hurried along the wall. He could breathe again, he was safe, but he knew that, just like the time he'd been pulled into the centre of the elephant procession, he'd been taken far away into a mysterious place inside himself.

Ben saw a few tourists and slowed. He brushed the mud off his legs. As he came around a corner he was close to the front entrance with its high steps and the porch with the rows of shoes and the blind guard. At the top of the stairs, to Ben's astonishment, the guard was holding out Ben's runners. A blind man had found his shoes. How could you explain that?

Ben crossed the courtyard to where the dusty elephant was still pulling at the chain that held his foot. How long was it since he'd stood there and fed straw to the elephant? Was it still afternoon?

Ben stared at the elephant's dark eyes. They seemed remarkably like the powerful eyes of the stone Ganesh inside the temple. Was some part of this small elephant linked to the statue? Could it be that the stone Ganesh moved his trunk to show him the way out because he'd fed this poor chained elephant? Did such things happen?

Ben picked up more straw and watched the elephant chew. He ran his hand over the warm swaying trunk. There was a connection. He could feel it.

Ben knew he had to get back to the hotel and said a sad farewell to the elephant. He hurried along the twisting streets hoping he'd remember the way. Then, ahead of him, down a lane Ben saw Gran with the Bonders, and he began to run. His grandmother looked goofy in her Tilley hat, and Geoffrey was even goofier in his bulging fishing vest, but since they were the only people he knew in Varanasi, Ben felt like crying with relief.

Gran was red in the face. "Ben, where have you been? What's the mark on your forehead?"

Before he could answer she grabbed him by his shoulder and shook him. "I'm furious with you, Ben. You've been gone for hours. How could you worry me like this?"

Ben realized he must still be breathing hard because no words came out.

Geoffrey pointed to a bench in a small park. "Sit down. Let's hear your explanation."

Gran was angry. "He'd better have a good one."

Ben studied his shoes as though he'd never seen them before. How could he explain something he didn't understand himself?

Gran didn't give him a chance. "Ben, I told you not to leave the hotel. I've been frantic. Thank heavens I had the Bonders to help me. We went all the way back to the river searching for you."

Geoffrey was angry too. "You owe your grandmother an explanation, young man."

Ben could hear his voice shaking. "I wanted to see the temple elephant again. I wanted to see if I could find someone to unchain his leg."

He explained how he'd followed the crowd to the temple porch, how he'd found himself handing his runners to the blind man, and how, without ever making a decision, he'd been swept into the temple. He told them about the dark passages and the Black Kali and the burning coals and the priest. He tried to describe the smells and the loud drumming that had made it impossible to think. He tried to explain how he'd felt as if he were far away, that he'd been pulled to a place he didn't understand.

Then he told them about the alcove with Ganesh and how the stone trunk of the statue had seemed to move to point the way out. How it *had* been the way out, a passage he'd never have found himself. Then how he'd found himself standing on grass at the back of the temple.

Gran and Martha and Geoffrey stared at him. Then Geoffrey spoke. "Do you realize we'd never have come looking for you *inside* a temple? Do you know how foolish you've been, what a risk you took?"

"I'm sorry."

"Ben, you disobeyed me when I specifically told you not to go out," said Gran. And then she stopped and put her arms around Ben and squeezed him tightly. "I'm so relieved you're safe."

Ben allowed himself to be hugged for a minute, then backed away. No matter how good they felt, public hugs from a grandmother were embarrassing.

Geoffrey went to a nearby drink stand and came back with cold sodas for everyone.

Ben took a drink. "I'm sorry I worried all of you. But it was amazing the way Ganesh rescued me. I saw the statue's trunk move. I know I did."

"You've got some imagination, young man," Geoffrey said.

Gran was thoughtful. "I'm not so certain. Strange things seem to happen in India." Then, to Ben's disgust, she spat on her handkerchief and tried to remove the mark on his fore-head. He ducked and used the back of his hand to rub at the spot himself.

Gran ignored him and spoke to the Bonders. "Don't know how I'd have managed without you, but now Ben and I have to get something to eat and find our way to the Old Vishnu guest house. Let's all meet later for dinner."

The cycle rickshaw driver in front of the hotel spoke good English. "Most certainly I know the Old Vishnu guest house," he said, showing them to their double seat before jumping on his bicycle and heading up the street. His skinny legs pedalled furiously until he stopped in front of a large house on a street close to the centre of town.

Ben was excited and led Gran up to the doorway and rang the brass bell. The woman who answered told them she didn't take in guests anymore. Her parents, she said, had been the original owners of the lodge. No one called Mukherjee had ever owned it.

Ben could see Gran was close to tears.

"You must not mind," said their rickshaw driver. "I know of two more guest homes with the name Vishnu. There is the New Vishnu and the Real Vishnu. I am being certain that one of them will be the place you seek."

Ben thought that every second lodge in the city must be called Vishnu. It was now mid-afternoon, and they had another long ride to the New Vishnu guest home, which was a small house with no sign.

At the front door, Ben nudged his grandmother. "This has gotta be it."

Gran introduced herself to a young woman and her husband at the door who shook their heads. "Very sorry, Mrs. Leeson. We purchased the home from a couple who came from Kerala in the south." The couple didn't know who'd owned the house before them, nor did they have a forwarding address.

Ben felt as though he'd been kicked in the stomach. If he were his father he'd be saying "Damn."

"Thank you for your trouble," Gran said. This time Gran just seemed old and tired when she got back into the rickshaw. The plastic seat had been in the burning sun too long and it felt like sitting on a hot iron. Ben almost wished he hadn't converted his long pants to shorts.

"Do not be discouraged," their driver said, calling over his shoulder, pedalling fast. "I am certain this next place which has nice bungalows will be the place you seek." After half an hour they reached the outskirts of the city where a row of new wooden cottages sat at the edge of a park. A sign said: THE REAL VISHNU GUEST BUNGALOWS.

"The poor man has been working hard to bring us all this way," Gran said.

"And this is our last hope," Ben said.

Gran mopped her brow as she got down from the rickshaw. "This looks like the kind of place an older couple would retire to. I can just imagine Shanti coming to visit here with her children and grandchildren."

Gran told her story to the young man who opened the door, but before she was finished the owner shook his head. "Madam, the friends you seek could not be living here. You see, these fine bungalows are new, finished only last year, and my father and I are the first owners. Perhaps you could try the Vishnu Lodge near the river."

"But that's the place we're staying!" Ben said. His heart sank. They'd come full circle. Their last hope in Varanasi had evaporated.

Ben realized how tired he was. Gran must be even more

worn out. The day had started at dawn after their sleepless night on the hard train bunks, then there had been the boat trip on the Ganges, Ben's terrifying time in the temple and Gran's search for him and now this hopeless ride across town and back.

Back in the guest house, Gran sank in her seat in front of a cup of tea. "Well, that's that. The search in India is over. We have nowhere else to go."

"Maybe not, Gran. You never know." It was hard, but Ben kept his promise to himself not to tell his grandmother about the message he'd left on the school site. If it didn't work out, he wouldn't have caused her another disappointment.

Gran took a last swallow of her tea and stared into space. "I'm sorry I brought you on this wild goose chase. I'm a stupid old woman."

It was terrible to see his grandmother so discouraged. "Remember what Padam told us about Gandhi, Gran. Patience and persistence."

Gran gave Ben a weak smile. "I remember Madhu teasing Padam that he didn't have much of either. But now there's nowhere else for us to look, Ben. You know, if I could change our tickets today and go back home, I would."

Ben realized he was ready to go home too.

Once Geoffrey Bonder saw Gran and Ben's faces, he didn't need to ask their news.

Over dinner, Martha, who had changed into another long,

flowered skirt, asked, "What will you do now?"

"Frankly, I don't know," Gran said.

"Why not forget your search and just enjoy India? Be tourists like us?" Martha said. "We just came from a beach town called Mahabalipuram."

"There are so many carved temples that it's been declared a world heritage site," Geoffrey added. He rummaged through his vest pockets until he found a card. "Here's where we stayed. The Ideal Beach House."

Ben perked up. "Good swimming?"

"Fabulous swimming in the Bay of Bengal," Martha said.

Gran was thoughtful. "Maybe that's what we need, Ben. We've got eleven more days before we fly back, and a stay near the beach sounds like heaven."

"It's just an hour by plane to Madras and then an hour by taxi south of there. You could be there tomorrow afternoon," Geoffrey said.

"What do you think, Ben? Should we go to the beach?"

"As we say in India, no problem."

Later that evening Gran was lying down in their room. "We've come to a complete dead end. It's like the game of Snakes and Ladders we used to play when you were little. You and I have been climbing ladders and sliding down one snake after another until we're right back where we started."

She seemed so depressed that Ben could hardly wait to get out of the room. "I'd better email Mum and tell her what's happened," he said. "I saw an internet shop down the street."

"Come right back, Ben. When I woke up this morning and you weren't here and the desk clerk didn't know where you were, I thought I'd lost you. It was a terrible feeling. I'm responsible for you in India and you were simply gone."

On his way out the door, he said, "I won't be long, Gran. Don't worry."

In the internet shop, Ben took at seat in front of the only computer.

Dear Mum and Lauren

I got lost in a temple today. It's hard 2 explain but I think an elephant god saved my life. We've been looking for the place where Shanti's parents lived but nobody knows anything about them. It's my guess they were never here.

G2G Ben

Ben keyed in the URL of the school's site. It had been four days since he'd sent a message to the site and there was an excellent chance that by now someone would have answered. He had a lucky feeling. Ganesh had saved him in the temple today. They were definitely on the same wavelength. Shanti could be living somewhere near them right now. Gran was going to flip when he told her.

Ben waited for the site to come up. When it did, the screen read: No messages.

So much for Ganesh. Now he was the one who needed cheering up.

Day Seven

THEIR LOCAL PLANE left at eleven, and the small airline terminal was packed with people; men talked loudly in groups and women in flowing saris clustered together to chat, while children chased each other between the groups. Loud announcements crackled down from large speakers, and stale air hovered over the waiting room, grey and heavy with cigarette smoke. Gran found a seat and opened her book.

Too hot to sit, Ben wandered around. Under the backpack, his t-shirt stuck to his skin. His hair dripped, so he took his cap off and stuffed it in his pack. He checked to make sure the wallet was in his pocket, then shifted his pack again to flick the thermometer on the zipper. Forty-six degrees. This place was a steaming fire pit.

Ben dropped down hard into the seat beside his grandmother. "Did you ever smoke, Gran?"

His grandmother looked up from her book, her face wet with perspiration. "I'm sorry to admit it, but I did. I quit before your father was diagnosed."

"I guess my dad learned to smoke from you."

"Don't think I haven't felt guilty about that, Ben." She took a deep breath. "Any mother would."

"So it's your fault Dad died."

"Ben!" Gran said, shocked.

Knowing he was being mean, Ben still kept going. "You could have stopped him smoking. He was your son."

"A mother can't stop a grown child from doing anything they want to do." She wiped her forehead. "You should know that. You're still a teenager, and your mother can't stop you from wasting all your time at the computer."

Ben folded his arms across his chest, burying his fists in his armpits. He looked around the steamy room. This heat was unbearable. His father's death was unbearable. Everything was unbearable.

Neither Ben nor his grandmother spoke during the flight. The attendant passed lemon candies and Gran took four. As the pilot announced their descent, Ben had his first glimpse of the wide rim of the Bay of Bengal stretching across the horizon. The Ganges River emptied into this bay. This is where the ashes from the corpses he'd seen at Varanasi ended up. Everyone ended up dead. Everyone ever born would end up dead. Ben had never thought about it before, but it was a fact.

A sign said: WELCOME TO CHENNAI.

"Chennai? Where are we?" Gran asked. "I thought the plane was taking us to Madras. We've come to the wrong city!"

"Gran, you remember Madhu told us some cities have new names," Ben said. "Chennai is probably the new name for Madras."

"Let's hope so," Gran said. "Otherwise we're in big trouble."

Carrying their backpacks, Gran and Ben were the first out of the terminal to reach the row of waiting taxis. Ben stayed behind his grandmother, where he didn't have to watch the fanny pack bounce against her stomach.

"Funny," Gran said, calling back, "when I saw the taxis, I thought of Madhu and Padam."

Ben had thought about their two friends from Delhi too, but right now he was too hot and angry to agree with his grandmother about anything.

They found a taxi driver who assured them that Chennai was the new name for Madras and told them that the drive to Mahabalipuram would take two hours and would cost a thousand rupees.

Ben sat in the back seat beside his grandmother. He realized he'd have to find a computer as soon as he could. If

Madras was now called Chennai, maybe Calcutta had a new name too. If he'd been using the wrong name on the school site, it could explain why there'd been no response.

Gran, who seemed to feel she had to carry on a long conversation with everyone she met, had leaned forward to talk to the driver. "I'm not sure I pronounced the name of the place we're going properly. How do you say it?"

Her constant chatter was driving Ben crazy, but the driver seemed pleased to talk. "Here in India we say names just the way they are written. Maha-bali-purum."

"Maha-bali-purum," Gran repeated. "Maha-bali-purum, Maha-bali-purum."

Ben gritted his teeth. He'd hurl himself out the car door if she said it one more time.

The driver manoeuvred the taxi onto the first wide highway they'd seen in India. "Speaking of names," he said, "my name is Ashok, a name from the ancient Sanskrit language that means 'happy one.'"

Gran introduced herself and her silent grandson. My name is Ben, he said under his breath and it means "miserable one." Ben closed his eyes and tried to close his ears to his grandmother's endless babbling.

At last the taxi turned into the treed driveway that led to the Ideal Beach Resort where a circle of bungalows sat around a wide grassy garden. Beyond the bungalows, Ben could see the ocean.

Ashok stopped at the building marked "Office" and got

their backpacks from the trunk. As Ben was about to step out of the taxi he saw that Gran had left her hat on the floor of the back seat. Ben stared at the hat, paused, then closed the door, leaving the hat in the car. He picked up his backpack and said goodbye to the driver.

"Come on, Ben," Gran said, walking up the path. "Why are you so grumpy today?"

Ben didn't answer.

A tall young man came to the office door and answered Gran's query. "Of course we have room for you. No problem. We have a bungalow with two bedrooms that should suit you perfectly."

Apparently "no problem" was what everyone said in this part of India too.

The young man wore shorts and a white shirt and had a handsome face with a friendly smile. He told them he ran the resort with his mother and sister and his name was Prem Gurin.

Taking Gran's backpack, Prem led them across the grass to a small bungalow with a hammock swinging from the wide veranda. Inside were two bedrooms separated by a narrow hallway and an adjoining bathroom. Pale green bedspreads and white wicker furniture made Gran comment that this was very different from their other hotels.

"My mother is serving tea at our own bungalow in half an hour so please join us," Prem said before he left them.

Gran turned to Ben. "Your choice. Take the bedroom you want. And try to drop that bad mood."

Ben picked up his backpack and took it into the room on the far side of the bathroom. He unpacked, put what clean clothes he had into the top drawer of a dresser and sat on the bed. It was too lame for a boy his age to be travelling with his grandmother. Everything he'd done in India had been with old people, including that gross couple, Martha and Geoffrey. He should be having fun with kids his own age. The only good thing about this place was that he'd never have to see the silly Tilley hat again.

Ben lay back on the bed, clasped his hands behind his head and looked up. A small green lizard clung to the ceiling directly above him, not moving. If that lizard let go, it would drop right onto his face. Ben turned his head and rolled on his side, curling up like he always did in his own bed at home.

Right now Mum and Lauren would be sound asleep on the other side of the world. He pictured the two of them waking up and walking around the Vancouver house. It was strange to think that his father wouldn't be there, reading the newspaper or cooking up his favourite porridge. Would his father's spirit still be in the house? Would Lauren and Mum be able to sense it? What was a person's spirit anyway?

Again, as he had so often in the last months, Ben tried to recollect what his dad had looked like. In all this time, he simply hadn't been able to "see" his dad's face. Try as hard as he could, no picture of his father ever came into his head.

Then, staring at the ceiling, he realized he could see a face and it was his father. Dad was smiling his crooked smile. The picture was strong and clear, and with it came memories. Memories of standing at the bathroom sink while his dad shaved, of Dad letting Ben squirt the shaving cream on his own cheeks, of being lifted up so he could make funny faces in the mirror. "Now there's a handsome lad," his father would say.

Ben could smell the peppermint shaving cream; he could feel Dad's arms around him. His father was here with him in this room. Not like a ghost, but a real person. And then the familiar ache came back. It came when you believed that someone was still alive and you were with them, and then you shook yourself and remembered it wasn't real. The person was gone, and you had that awful hollow ache in your chest when you knew you'd never be able to see them or hear them or touch them again.

Ben didn't know what to do with the hurt. It almost stopped him from breathing, until, as always, it flipped and twisted into anger. He knew what to do with anger. His father had let him down. He used to think his dad was smart, but he'd been wrong. His dad hadn't been smart enough to quit smoking, not smart enough to make sure he'd be around when his son was growing up. Ben was burning up with anger and breathing hard.

He heard his grandmother call, "Are you going to stay in your bad mood forever or are you coming for tea?"

Ben grabbed the pillow and threw it across the room. The lizard scampered along the ceiling and disappeared behind the gauze curtain. Ben stood up and looked at himself in the mirror. Same old feelings, same old Ben. He ran a brush through his messed-up hair, rubbed his eyes with his knuckles and went down the hall and out the door calling to his grandmother, "Let's go."

Gran hurried after him across the lawn to the Gurins' bungalow.

Mrs. Gurin had a wide face and hair tied in a bun at the back of her head. She wore a white sari and Ben noticed a blue dot in the middle of her forehead as she introduced her daughter Rani, who came up behind her.

Ben found himself staring at the most beautiful girl he'd ever seen. Rani had a mark on her forehead like her mother, long loose dark hair and brown eyes that were almost too big for her face. She wore blue jeans and a white t-shirt, just like a Canadian girl.

"Why don't you two take some lemonade outside while we have tea?" Mrs. Gurin said.

Rani carried two glasses of lemonade and pointed to chairs on the porch. Neither Ben nor Rani spoke, and then they both talked at once.

"I'm wondering why you and your grandmother have come to India —"

"I can't believe everyone here speaks such good English—"

They laughed awkwardly and Ben said, "You first."

"We study English in school," Rani answered. "But here in Tamil Nadu, we speak Tamil. I am also studying Hindi. Your turn."

Ben smiled. "We're here because we're looking for someone who lives in India, but it isn't working out."

"Tell me about it." Rani leaned forward eagerly.

"Well, my grandmother is determined to find a woman called Shanti who used to be her pen pal. We've tried everything. We went to the registry office in Delhi, then two great taxi drivers took us to Agra and we found the street where Shanti's parents used to live. People told us they'd moved to Varanasi, so we took the overnight train and went all over town trying to find the right Vishnu Lodge. We went to four different places, all called Vishnu!" He stopped for breath.

Rani was laughing. She had the whitest teeth he'd ever seen. "I can believe it. Vishnu is a popular god."

"I figured that, but Gran was sure discouraged. She said coming to India was a stupid idea. Now she's given up, and that's why we're here. "

"Do *you* think coming to India was a stupid idea?"

"I don't know. I've seen some awesome things, but travelling with my grandmother bugs me sometimes. She talks too much to everyone we meet and she gets upset if I don't do everything the way she wants it done."

Rani seemed surprised. "That's not so bad. Prem and I have one grandmother and she lives in Darjeeling in the north. We can visit her only once a year."

"Being with a grandmother twenty-four hours a day is different from visiting," Ben said. "My grandmother'll spaz if I'm out of her sight for a minute."

"My mother has to know where I am too. I always ask her permission to go into town."

He didn't want Rani to think he was too critical of his grandmother. She should know he was an okay person. "I'm working on a way to find Shanti for Gran. I have a secret plan."

"Can you tell me?"

"Yep. I've put a message on the site of the school Shanti went to fifty years ago. I'm sure it will work because a woman we met in Delhi told us that's how former students get in touch with each other. I haven't told my grandmother because I want to surprise her."

"I've heard of those school sites. My brother will let you use the computer in the office." Rani stood and picked up their glasses.

Prem showed Ben the office computer and Rani sat beside him in front of the screen. "I think I know why this hasn't worked before," Ben said. "First I want to try something." He keyed in the site for the Calcutta Senior Girls' School.

"Any responses?" Rani said.

"No, not one. Tell me, is there a new name for Calcutta?"

"Yes, it was changed to match the languages spoken in our states. Calcutta's new name is Kolkota."

"I bet that's why I haven't had a response," Ben said. He decided to try searching for the school under Kolkota. He typed in Calcutta Girls' School but this time added Kolkota to his search terms, and found that yes, there was another website for the school. "CGS Alumni: Tell us what you think of our new website," read a message on the home page. The one he had used earlier must be an old one and had not yet been taken down. He wrote a new message asking any former students who knew Shanti to leave a message, and pressed Send. "That should do it!"

"Let's check tomorrow," Rani said. "Right now, how about coming with me to see the beach?"

"Awesome idea," Ben said. "I'll just tell Gran we're going."

"I'll tell my mother too. See you outside your bungalow in five minutes."

On the way to the beach, Rani was so friendly, Ben figured he could ask a question. "I was wondering about that round mark you have on your forehead?"

To his astonishment, she reached up and picked the blue dot off. "It's called a bindi. The old-fashioned way is to make a bindi with coloured powder. My mother does that, but most girls my age just use a coloured sticker. See?" She held out her finger with the paper dot.

"What does it mean?" he asked.

"It's a symbol of female energy. It protects girls and women. We buy these paper ones on sheets. Any colour you like to suit your mood!" Rani laughed. "Now, can I ask you a question?"

"Shoot."

"Are you a baseball player?"

"Sometimes." Ben was puzzled. "Oh, my baseball cap. I wear it to keep off the sun. And it's kind of a cool cap." Ben doffed it at Rani.

"You mean cool like not hot or cool like cool?"

"Both, I guess," Ben said.

"I like it," Rani said. "It is cool." That smile again.

They climbed over sand dunes and down onto the shore where they could see across the water to a red lighthouse at the farthest point of the headland. "You live in an amazing place. A beach like this is not what I expected in India," Ben said.

"What did you expect?"

"Absolutely nothing that I've found! Like, seeing a man levitate in the air. Like a stone statue that moved to show me the way out of a temple." Ben waved his arm like an elephant's trunk.

"A stone statue that moved?" Rani looked surprised.

"Yes, I swear it did. I saw it," Ben said.

"Quite a trip for someone your age!" Rani laughed. "You're my age, aren't you, Ben? I'm almost thirteen."

"I turned thirteen last year. You live with your parents?"

"Just my mum and my sister Lauren. She's nine. My dad died last March."

Rani was quiet for a moment. "Such a short time ago. My father died when I was two years old. My mother raised us." She bent to take off her sandals and bury her feet in the warm sand. A silver bracelet with tiny bells dangled from her ankle. Her legs were the colour of coffee with cream. "Prem is almost twenty now, but he is staying at home to help run the resort. I'd like to go to university and then travel when I graduate."

After wandering along the beach for a time, they headed back. Ben said, "I wish my PlayStation was working. I'd let you hear some cool music." He explained about needing an adapter.

"This town's not very big, but we might be able to get you one."

"I think my grandmother knew we could buy one in India, but she didn't tell me. I guess we all have our secrets." Ben shrugged his shoulders. "But it's no problem. I don't miss it much these days."

Back at the bungalow Gran was stretched out in the hammock, pushing her foot against the porch railing to keep it swinging. "You have fun with Rani? She seems like a lovely girl."

"She's okay."

Gran wobbled on the swinging hammock as she tried to get out. "I bet you're hungry. They don't serve dinner at the resort so we should go into town and find a place to eat."

Ben was hungry, and he didn't feel like talking on the walk into town. They passed shops with stone carvings in the windows and stopped at the market. Piles of melons, squash and oranges rose on counters above bins of rice and beans and wide baskets filled with cucumbers, tomatoes and purple eggplant. They wandered inside the covered market, where haunches of meat hung in rows in one corner. On the counter, a pile of orange meat was covered with whizzing flies. Ben's stomach lurched.

"We're a long way from the rows of wrapped meat at Safeway," Gran said.

"Yep. No sign of refrigeration," Ben said. "Let's get out of here."

Up the street, they found a small restaurant. It seemed clean, but after the gross displays at the market, Ben had decided never to eat meat again. He ordered dhal and rice with chapatis.

Gran ordered goat curry. "Never eaten goat, but I hear it's good."

"Yuck!"

"We'll see," Gran said.

The curry came in a heaped bowl of brown blobs floating in dark gravy. It was a silent meal. Ben didn't have anything to say, and Gran seemed absorbed in her own thoughts. Ben wondered how soon she'd miss her hat. They finished the meal quickly, and as they got up Ben saw that Gran had a dribble of brown on her chin.

"You've got goat gravy on your face, Gran," Ben said. Gran wiped with her paper napkin but didn't get it all. What did it matter.

Silently they passed through the darkening town back to their bungalow. The sun had just sunk and left behind a streaky purple sky over a dark and sombre sea.

They were a long way from home.

Day Eight

BEN OPENED HIS EYES. The sound of retching from the bathroom had woken him. Over the steady pulse of the large ceiling fan, he could hear his grandmother vomiting.

Ben leapt out of bed and stood barefoot outside their adjoining bathroom door. "Are you okay, Gran?"

"I hope so," was the hoarse response. Then a pause. "Must be . . . that curry I had last night." Another pause, then more retching. "*You're* not sick are you, Ben?"

"No, I'm just tired," Ben answered. Not certain what to do, Ben waited, standing by the door.

White and shaky, his grandmother opened the door. Clutching her nightgown across her stomach, she stumbled back to bed.

"It's cramps . . . like knives . . . one after another," she groaned. Ben helped her onto the bed, where she lay doubled up on her side with her face buried in the pillow.

Her voice was weak. "I feel so awful. I never should have brought you to India. It's all hopeless."

"Oh, Gran, I know we ran into a dead end in Varanasi, but don't worry about that now." This was not the time to tell her that this could be the day there'd be a message on the school site.

"I'm a stupid old woman. Thinking I could find someone I knew fifty years ago." Gran interrupted herself and rushed back to the bathroom. There were more sounds of heaving.

It sounded gross in there. She'd need water. Ben poured some from the pitcher on the dresser and sat waiting on the end of his grandmother's bed. When Gran came unsteadily out of the bathroom, she sat down beside him. Her hands were shaking as she sipped the water. Then she dropped back on the bed. One second later she was gagging and struggling to get up. There was no time to shut the bathroom door before she was vomiting in even more violent spasms.

This had to be malaria. Gran was always reminding him to take his pills, but he'd never asked if she was taking hers. He sat on the bed, listening for sounds from the bathroom and keeping his bare feet off the floor in case of lizards or cockroaches.

When she shuffled out of the bathroom, Gran was stooped over like a one-hundred-year-old woman. Ben shivered. He could tell she was going to die.

Gran collapsed on the bed, barely able to raise her head from the pillow. "Don't worry, Ben . . . it's called Delhi belly . . . food poisoning . . . work its way through."

"I thought you'd missed taking your pills and you got malaria."

"I've . . . been . . . taking the . . . pills."

"More water, Gran?" offered Ben.

"No. Couldn't keep . . . down. Go back to bed . . . I'll sleep."

Ben gave his grandmother a last look and turned out the light. "I'll leave the door between our rooms open, Gran."

Ben lay down on his own bed. He wasn't sure if he'd done the right thing leaving Gran. It was all so weird. The last thing he remembered was listening hard, not sure if he was imagining the soft scurrying noises in the room. Who knew what crawling creatures were hiding in the darkness? Who knew what would happen to his grandmother? He'd never seen anyone as sick as she was. And she was so weak. If she died, he'd be by himself, all alone in India.

Then he heard more vomiting. Ben sat up, acutely awake. Rushing to the bathroom door Ben saw his grandmother collapsed on the tile floor.

"Can't get up . . ." It was an effort for Gran to speak. "Can't stop . . . get a doctor, Ben."

Still in his pajamas and bare feet, Ben ran out into the dark, across the wet grass to the Gurins' bungalow. He pounded on the door with both hands. After a few long moments, a sleepy Prem opened the door.

Ben could barely catch his breath. "It's my grandmother. She's been vomiting all night. Can you find a doctor?"

Prem put his hand on Ben's shoulder and said, "No problem, Ben. I'll phone the doctor in town right away. Go back and stay with your grandmother."

Ben raced back across the grass, only faintly aware of the sun just rising over the rim of the sea. His grandmother was still lying on the bathroom floor. She had crawled close to the wall and lay curled up like a little kid. In her rumpled nightgown she could have been one of the bodies on the street in Delhi.

The body moaned and Ben knelt down beside her. "The doctor's coming, Gran."

A few minutes later Prem came in and said, "The doctor will arrive in fifteen minutes. He lives close by and will come on his bicycle."

Prem's eyes opened wide when he saw Gran slumped on the bathroom floor. He signalled to Ben. "We must get your grandmother up."

With Prem lifting Gran's shoulders and Ben holding her bare legs, they managed to lift her onto the bed. Prem was wiping Gran's face with a wet cloth when a bearded man in a high blue turban arrived. To Ben's relief, the man spoke English. Prem introduced Ben.

"Hello, Ben. I am Dr. Sandeep Dhaliwal. Prem told me your grandmother has been sick all night. Vomiting and diarrhea, correct?"

Ben nodded. The doctor bent over Gran and asked, "When were you first sick, Mrs. Leeson?"

"About eleven last night . . . it got worse."

The doctor was taking Gran's pulse.

"What is it?" Ben asked.

"Probably food poisoning. This can happen in India," said Dr. Dhaliwal.

"My grandmother had goat curry last night. That was it!" said Ben.

"We rarely find out what causes the food poisoning," said Dr. Dhaliwal. He felt Gran's forehead, shook down a thermometer and put it in her mouth.

"She has a bit of a fever," he said. He leaned over the bed. "Mrs. Leeson, you are dehydrated from the fluids you've lost. I'd like to put you in hospital and start a saline drip."

Ben's worst fears were coming true. His grandmother had a fever. She was dehydrated. She was so sick she had to go to a hospital. An Indian hospital! Was that man in a turban a qualified doctor?

"I'll phone for an ambulance," Prem said, and with a nod from Dr. Dhaliwal, he was out the door.

The doctor put down his stethoscope. "Ben, pack a bag for your grandmother. Put in her toothbrush and clean nightclothes."

"I will," Ben said. "And her malaria pills and her high-blood pressure pills too."

"Good man. We'll make sure she gets those." Dr. Dhaliwal

sat at the end of the bed holding Gran's wrist while Ben rushed to gather the things from the bathroom.

"Tell me what brings you and your grandmother to India," he asked Ben.

Ben stood by the bed, gripping the backpack to his chest. Trying to hide his shaky voice, he told the doctor about their search for Shanti. Being scared always made his voice wobble.

"That's an interesting quest," Dr. Dhaliwal said. "What was the pen pal's name?"

"We don't know her married name. When she wrote to my grandmother her name was Shanti Mukherjee."

Dr. Dhaliwal packed up his medical equipment. "It may be a coincidence, but I knew a man in Calcutta called Mukherjee. You see, although I am from the Punjab, I won a scholarship to medical school in Calcutta, and it is there I met a fellow student who may be related to the woman you seek."

Just then Prem came to the door with two men in white shirts, carrying a stretcher between them. They lifted Ben's grandmother onto the canvas stretcher and tightened a strap across the middle. It was awful to see Gran lying there with her face screwed up in pain.

Ben thought he should reassure her about the money and he leaned over to whisper, "I'll take care of the money, Gran. I'll wear the fanny pack."

"Thank . . . you," she sighed, not opening her eyes.

Ben squeezed her hand and followed the group as it trekked back across the lawn. Overlapping footprints in the morning's wet grass had kept a visible record of the procession of people who had crossed it, beginning with Ben's barefoot race in the dark to get Prem.

The sun was now up, and Ben's watch said almost eight o'clock. "Can I come in the ambulance?" he asked the attendant who was loading the end of the stretcher.

"Sorry, no one rides in here except us," the attendant said as he closed the door.

"I'll meet you at the hospital," said Dr. Dhaliwal to the attendants. "Ben, you come to the hospital with Prem after four this afternoon. It's my guess that you'll find your grandmother feeling a good deal better." The ambulance pulled out along the gravel driveway, giving Ben no time to protest.

He hadn't even had a chance to say goodbye to his grandmother. A terrible feeling washed over him. He remembered Geoffrey Bonder telling the joke about the sick man taking one look at the entrance of an Indian hospital and announcing he was cured.

What had he done, letting his grandmother be taken to a hospital in India? He'd been irresponsible. His father would never have done that. Dad was always so good at taking care of things. Ben thought he'd probably find his grandmother's cold dead body when he got to the hospital.

Prem put his arm around Ben's shoulder. "Cheer up, old boy. Let's get some breakfast into you. I can smell my mother's dosas cooking."

"I'd better email my mother and tell her what's happened," Ben said. He had to swallow hard to get the wobble out of his voice.

"Why not wait until after we've been to the hospital this afternoon? We'll have a better idea later of how your grandmother is recovering. These bugs usually work their way out. No need to alarm anyone just yet."

Rani and her mother sat across the table from Prem and Ben. The fried crepes filled with vegetables were hot and spicy, but Ben was distracted, imagining his grandmother being injected with dirty needles. She'd be scared. She didn't know one person in the hospital. He refused the second masala dosa Rani offered him.

"I'm sure my grandmother's sick because she ate goat curry last night," Ben said.

"What makes you think it was the goat meat?" Mrs. Gurin asked.

"Gran and I were at the market yesterday. None of that meat is refrigerated."

"True," Mrs. Gurin said, "but it's fresh. Did you see the bright orange meat?"

"Sure did. Gran couldn't believe it."

"That's goat meat!" said Rani, smiling. "It's orange before it's cooked. Here we mostly eat vegetarian meals, but snake meat and goat meat are sold in our markets."

Rani and Prem laughed at the look on Ben's face.

"Your grandmother is overtired," Mrs. Gurin said. "This trip has been upsetting for her."

Ben shook his head. You don't get so sick just from being overtired. It was scary that she could be so weak so fast. Maybe Gran was wrong about taking her malaria pills. Maybe she'd forgotten she'd missed one. Or maybe they weren't working. People died from malaria. Ben felt as though a monster had tied a rope around his chest and was pulling on it. "Gran could have malaria."

"No. She doesn't have any symptoms of malaria," Prem said.

"Don't worry, Ben," Rani said. "Your grandmother is in good hands. Let the hospital take care of her."

Rani asked her mother something in a language Ben couldn't understand. Mrs. Gurin nodded. "I've just asked my mother if I could take you swimming this morning after I do my work," Rani said.

When she looked directly at you, Rani's dark eyes danced with light. He'd never seen eyes like them. For a moment Ben forgot to answer. Then he said, "Great idea, but I have to be at the hospital by four o'clock."

"Tell you what," Prem said. "I have work to do in the office and Rani's helping the women who clean the resort. Why don't you make up for the sleep you lost last night, and Rani can come for you at eleven."

"Excellent," agreed Ben.

"Bring a towel," Rani called as she headed out the door to start work.

Once again Ben crossed the grass, now beginning to

vibrate with the heat of the morning sun. The bungalow showed signs of a hard night. Sheets trailed off his grandmother's rumpled bed; towels were scattered around the bathroom. The memory of his grandmother slumped on the floor made Ben feel sick. He had the whole day to put in before he could see her at the hospital. His head buzzed; he was wide awake.

Poor Gran. She'd had been in agony, and he'd stood by uselessly. He was not a good grandson. He'd left her favourite hat in the taxi and not said a word. Before that he'd blamed her for his father's smoking. That was unfair. People started smoking because they didn't know any better, and then they were hooked. His dad had tried to quit, but it was too late.

Ben picked up Gran's guidebook and sat on his own bed. Once more he studied the elephant photograph on the cover, then he flipped through a few pages. He lay back on the bed and started reading about the maharaja rule in India.

The next thing he heard was Rani calling his name at the bungalow door. "Ben! Wake up. It's time to swim."

Ben tried to make his voice sound as though he hadn't been asleep. "Be right there. Just changing into my bathing suit."

He decided he had to take the fanny pack with him to the beach so he rolled it in a towel and put it under his arm. When he came out he saw that Rani wore a loose cotton beach coat over her dark blue bathing suit and had a towel over her shoulder. And she was smiling at him. "Race you!" she called.

Ben stowed the towel under a palm tree and was first into the warm water, but once there Rani matched him stroke for stroke. Every few minutes Ben looked up to check that his towel with the money was safe under the tree. Rani and Ben chased each other through the water, dived for shells and hurled themselves through the waves. Ben lay on his back, buoyed up by the salty green water, and for the first time since he'd come to India, felt completely relaxed.

When they came out of the water, Rani put on her beach coat and they sat under the tree watching men cast fishing lines from the two catamarans floating offshore. It all seemed unreal. Was it really Ben Leeson sitting beside a girl on a white sand beach in India? His old life in Vancouver felt a world away. Of course when you thought about it, Vancouver *was* half a world away.

Then he remembered Gran. "Tell me about Dr. Dhaliwal," he asked Rani. "He said he was from the Punjab. Where's that?"

"The Punjab is a state in the north where most Sikhs live, though many Sikhs live here in Tamil Nadu too. I believe Dr. Dhaliwal did his residency here and fell in love with Mahabalipurum. The doctor and his family are a respected part of our community."

"Is he a good doctor?"

"Oh, yes, your grandmother is fortunate to be in his care."

"I hope so. It just seemed strange to have a doctor wearing a turban."

"I can see it would seem strange to you. I'm thinking you must be Christian, Ben?" Rani asked.

"Well, sort of. We're Unitarian, which is kind of a non-religion, but Lauren and I went to Sunday school for a couple of years. I never thought about religion until I got over here where it's so important. What about you? You're Hindu, aren't you?"

"Yes, I am."

"You must believe in reincarnation?"

"Yes, we believe that when we die our souls are reborn and we come back to earth as other people."

"Really?"

"And we return many times until we reach enlightenment. It might take thousands of years."

"You mean a person could come back and live other lives?"

"Yes."

Ben picked up a fistful of sand and tossed it in the air. "I just can't go for that. It's too weird."

Rani didn't say anything. Ben picked up another handful of sand. "I'd like to believe that a person's soul or their spirit could live on, but not inside another person. Say my father came back as someone else. I'd recognize him, wouldn't I? If the person had my dad's soul, I think I'd know." He dropped the sand.

"You shouldn't be so quick to judge."

"The reincarnation stuff is just too crazy for me to believe."

Rani stood up. "Ben, I'm not saying you have to believe." She looked angry and turned away in the direction of the bungalows.

Ben hurried after her. He'd made her mad; he was just like Gran who'd judged Shanti about her arranged marriage. He called, "Rani, I'm sorry. Please wait."

Ben caught up to her. "I'm a lame jerk. Sorry if I seemed to be criticizing your beliefs. I'm just trying to figure it all out. I need to know what happens when someone dies. There's got to be more than being buried and eaten by worms or burned and turned into ashes. Tell me about what you believe."

Rani nodded. "It's hard to understand another culture and hard for me to explain. Hinduism is complicated."

They reached a shady bench under a row of large trees and sat down.

"Have you heard about karma?" Rani asked. "It's something else for you to think about."

"What's karma?" Ben asked.

Rani took a breath. "In our religion everyone is responsible for their own behaviour. Karma is what comes from our actions. Good ones and bad ones. The deeds people do in their lifetimes determine their destiny in the next life."

Ben thought about it. Of course. It made sense that you were responsible for the way you behaved in life. In a flash he saw the rumpled Tilley hat lying in the taxi. The skin on his back prickled. He'd simply walked away and left it there. What kind of a deed was that? Then into his mind came the picture of strangers carrying his grandmother's stretcher through the door of the hospital. Right at this moment, while he was sitting here talking to Rani, Gran could be dying.

Rani's voice interrupted his thoughts. "I can see you're worried about your grandmother."

"Yep."

"Ben, it's a fine hospital. Last year I had my appendix taken out there."

"You did? You seem to have survived okay." He'd never get tired of a smile like that. "You know there's another thing. I've been mean to my grandmother ever since we left Varanasi. I feel terrible about it."

"Being mean hasn't made her sick, Ben," Rani said.

"What if she dies?"

"She won't. Just tell her you're sorry when you see her."

"I'm not so mad anymore. It was stupid of me. I blamed her for my dad dying, because she didn't make him stop smoking. It wasn't her fault."

A burst of fresh wind off the ocean travelled across the grass. It stirred the palms, rustling the long branches and clearing away the guilty storm in Ben's head. He knew what to do. "I'll get my grandmother a new hat in town."

"Does she need a new hat?" Rani asked.

"Yes, if I'm going to have some good karma," Ben answered.

"Always a good idea," Rani said.

He couldn't believe how fast time passed when he and Rani talked. She seemed to have forgiven him for being critical of her beliefs and was back to being friendly. Ben checked his watch. "Almost time to go to the hospital. I'd better get ready."

In the bungalow the sheets were pulled tight across Gran's bed; the afternoon breeze billowed the white curtains halfway across the room. Ben put on a clean shirt and was waiting by Prem's car before four o'clock.

Prem drove along the dusty streets, past the shops lining the main road to the three-storey brick hospital on the other side of the village. Ben was nervous, not knowing what he'd find as he neared the stone entrance.

Inside, it smelled like the hospital where his father had surgery. Prem asked one of the nurses hurrying along the hall where they could find Norah Leeson. She pointed to a long room with frosted windows and rows of beds. A nursing sister took them to the far end of the room near the nursing station.

The first sight of his grandmother scared Ben. She seemed to have shrunk and lay with her eyes closed, her arms stretched out along her body. A white sheet was pulled up tightly to her chin. From a bottle above the bed, a tube led to a needle in the back of her hand.

"How are you, Gran?" said Ben, bending over. "It's me."

Gran opened her eyes. "Oh, Ben. Good to see you."

She shifted her head on the pillow. "The nurses here are taking good care of me, and Dr. Dhaliwal is an excellent doctor."

"I was worried." Ben grabbed his grandmother's free hand.

Gran reached up and stroked Ben's cheek. "Have you been all right without me?"

"Yes, I'm with Prem and Rani. I haven't emailed Mum yet because I wanted to wait until I'd seen you. I'll do it tonight." He squeezed hard on Gran's hand. "I feel terrible, Gran."

"You haven't lost the money, have you?"

"It's in your fanny pack, right here. See?" Ben patted his waist. He had to wear it and Prem hadn't said anything about it. Ben was getting up his courage to explain to his grandmother that it was her hat he was feeling terrible about, when a nurse came by and reported that Dr. Dhaliwal was pleased at how Mrs. Leeson was responding to treatment. There had been no more diarrhea or vomiting and the intravenous drip was working. She added, "Because of her age the doctor wants your grandmother to stay overnight to get her strength back."

"Ben can stay with us, Mrs. Leeson," Prem said. "We'll take good care of him."

"Thank you, Prem," Gran said, her eyes closing.

"Visiting hours start again at four o'clock tomorrow. I'll be here, Gran." Ben gave her hand a final squeeze, but it seemed his grandmother was already asleep.

On the way home, Prem stopped at the market to buy fish and vegetables for his mother to make a curry. Ben bought a green baseball cap that said DELHI DEVILS over the visor.

When they got back to the resort, Prem went into his bungalow with the groceries and Ben went into the office to use the computer. Surely there would be a message on the school site finally to cheer up Gran. First he'd email home.

> Dear Mum and Lauren
>
> Gran got food poisoning and she couldn't get up from the bathroom floor. I think it's from goat curry even though nobody else does. Her doctor has a long beard and wears a turban. Don't believe what U hear about Indian hospitals. This 1 is very clean. The doctor says Gran is getting better.
>
> G2G Ben
> p.s. Don't worry about me. I'll never eat goat curry.

Then he keyed in the school address. The screen flashed, then: No Messages. He'd been so certain this time. Ben turned off the computer and left the room.

Rani met him at the door. "Any luck?"

"No, and I was sure there would be a message."

"Well, do you know what Gandhi said?"

"Yes, everyone in India knows. Patience and persistence!"

"We must remember that." Rani smiled.

On the way to the Gurins' bungalow, Rani asked, "I was wondering if you play chess?"

"My dad did start to teach me, but I can hardly remember," Ben said.

"I could teach you."

"You're on! Thanks."

Rani won both games, but the second one was close. After the fish curry dinner, they played another game. "You're a fast learner," said Rani. "By the way, I have permission from my mother to take you to see the cobra farm near here tomorrow."

"Cobra farm?"

"Yes, it's famous. They milk the cobras for live venom and make an antidote to save the lives of people bitten by cobras."

"Wicked!" exclaimed Ben.

Rani laughed. "We can swim first and go on bikes. I'll lend you a spare one we have here."

"Sweet," Ben said.

"Sweet! Wicked! We don't use those strange words in India," Rani said, laughing again.

"That's the way kids talk back in Canada."

"It's like a special language," Rani said, laughing.

Feeling brave, Ben turned down the offer of a bed in Prem's room, assuring the family he'd be fine in the bungalow not too far away.

Somehow the bungalow didn't seem quite as safe as it had when he and Gran first arrived. Ben turned on the light and leapt into bed as fast as he could. He thought about the visit to the cobra farm. He wrapped the covers around his shoulders. If there were cobras so near, who's to say there wasn't one curled up in the corner or climbing onto the end of this bed? What are you supposed to do if you have a cobra in your bed?

Ben told himself not to be a jerk. He was thirteen, old enough to go to India. He was old enough to take care of himself.

Day Nine

"WHY DO ALL THE bungalows have this raised step in the doorway?" Ben asked.

"It's to keep scorpions and other crawlers out," Rani said.

"You mean snakes? A snake could crawl over it?" Ben asked.

"Guess so. And it could crawl all over YOU!" she said, running away, her dark hair flying out behind her.

Ben had the fanny pack wrapped in his towel again where he could see it from the water. The swimming was even more fun than the day before. When they were too tired to jump the waves anymore, Rani suggested they build sand temples.

"Sand temples? I'm there!" Ben said.

On their hands and knees, they cleared a wide area, scooping up the top sand to get at the deeper wet sand. Then, like six-year-olds, they set to work. Gulls cried out in a shrill chorus above them, and gusts of wind flicked at the tops of waves, throwing cool water along their backs.

"How's that?" Rani said, leaning back to admire her creation.

What Rani had built was like no other sandcastle Ben had ever seen. A large dome with towers on the corners, it was just like the Taj Mahal.

"It's awesome," he said.

"Yours is like an English castle," Rani said.

"I guess it is," said Ben. He'd never seen an English castle and wondered why, like every other kid in Canada, he'd always built a sandcastle that looked like one.

Rani put the finishing touches on the river behind her temple. "Tell me about your school."

"Not much to tell. The kids are okay. A few of the guys are into cigarettes or dope. I'm not." Ben sat back on his knees.

"It's good you don't want to smoke."

"Yep. I worry I might have inherited the smoking genes from my dad. Anyway, it doesn't appeal to me."

"Me either," Rani said. She thought for a minute. "I guess you have girls at your school?"

"Yep, but we don't talk much," Ben answered.

"Mine is a residential school. It's all girls, so I don't talk to boys at all."

"But you're so easy to talk to."

"You too," Rani said. She gave Ben a shy smile. "You know Indian girls are often chaperoned when they're with a boy. I'm lucky my mother lets me go with you to show you around."

"My grandmother hasn't been letting me go anywhere on my own until we came here."

"Tell me about your mother."

"Oh, she's okay, but lately she's after me because I play computer games all the time. The games I like all have a kind of battle and a quest. You can spend hours playing them, but when I think about it now, they're sort of lame compared to this real life search for Shanti. I just wish someone from Shanti's school would answer my email."

"I have an idea, Ben," Rani said. "Do you know about Ganesh?"

"I do. I like Ganesh. In fact, he's the god who showed me the way out of the temple where I was lost in Varanasi."

"Ganesh has already helped you then!" Rani said.

"It felt like we connected." Ben smoothed the sand in the moat around his castle.

Rani said, "Lots of young people in India call on Ganesh for help to overcome obstacles."

"How do they do that?"

Rani seemed pleased with herself. "I'll show you when we get to town."

"Hindus have so many gods and goddesses. The temple I was lost in was Black Kali's temple."

"How scary for you! Kali is frightening."

"Why do you have a goddess like that? A goddess of destruction with blood and everything?"

"Well, Christians have a hell, and as I understand it, there is a red devil that is scary. And people can burn in hell."

"Sure, but most people think they won't go there."

"Right, and I guess Kali scares people into being good."

"Worked for me. I've been good. Most of the time," Ben said, and they both laughed.

Ben brushed the sand off his hands and got out his camera. "Wait a minute. I want to take pictures of your sand temple . . . and you."

Ben showed Rani the photographs on his memory card. She liked the ones of the Red Fort and the ghats at Varanasi, and she agreed that the poor elephant outside the Kali temple looked neglected. "You've got some good pictures there, Ben," Rani said.

"Hope so. I have to put them into a project for school when I get home."

Later they went to the resort office so Ben could check his email. Again, even with the new website, the screen showed the disappointing: No Messages. That was the end of the trail. If no one had contacted him by now, it meant that there was no one out there who knew Shanti.

He might as well forget about finding her. Maybe now he could tell Gran he'd been trying, but not until four o'clock when he saw her again. As he sat there, a new message popped up. It was from his mother.

> Hi Ben!
>
> Thanks for your email. I'm proud of you for looking after Gran. Hope you aren't lonely when she's in the hospital. We've had nothing but snow here the past two days. Lauren says to tell you her hockey team made the semi-finals.
>
> Hugs and kisses
> Mum

Ben had a funny cut-off feeling after reading his mother's message. It gave him a nervous flutter in his stomach. He could see the North Shore mountains covered in snow. And the snow in their front yard. The house always looked so tidy against all the whiteness. He could see his mother's face, feel her smooth cheek when she hugged him. He really was far away — far away from his mother, from the snow and from her hugs.

With Gran in the hospital, he was more or less taking care of himself. That was fine. He could do it. Gran would be better soon, and in a week, they'd be flying home.

Ben put on the fanny pack and rushed to meet Rani. She'd probably think he looked ridiculous.

But Rani didn't comment on it when she saw him, just showed him a bike and asked if he was ready to see cobras. He was. Rani led the way as they cycled through the town and onto a bumpy gravel road. The road wound past small farm houses with goats tethered in the yard and children playing in the shade of coconut trees. She signalled to Ben. "We turn here."

On either side of the narrow path, long fan-shaped leaves flopped through the undergrowth onto the trail. Overhead, tall trees blocked the sun. The chattering of parrots filled the air, and Ben caught flashes of their bright green plumage, like Christmas lights, up among the branches.

"Up there," Rani said, pointing to the tallest trees. "See the family of howler monkeys?"

Ben heard the monkeys before he saw them. Their deep whoops and howls echoed across the swaying treetops. Ben counted eight monkeys of all sizes swinging from branch to branch, one arm stretching over the other and their long curled tails acting as a third arm. His bike wobbled as he tried to watch the monkeys overhead and navigate the narrow path at the same time.

Then Rani stopped at a grassy clearing and pointed to some clay-coloured rocks. Beside the rocks, three men crouched on the ground, giving their attention to something between them.

"They're the venom collectors," Rani whispered. She and Ben lowered their bikes onto the grass and moved closer. One of the men held onto the mid-section of a cobra about two metres long. It had a thick body ringed with black and yellow bands and a creamy yellow underbelly. The snake's wide hood flared around its head. Ben saw a second man cupping his hand behind the hood with his fingers on either side of the cobra's head, immobilizing it.

"He presses milk out from the poison glands beside the eyes," said Rani.

Ben saw the snake's eyes flash. "Not a happy snake," he whispered.

A third man held a glass dish under the snake's open mouth. Ben saw the two pale fangs, like long hypodermic needles.

"Those fangs puncture the skin of a victim and the poison goes into their blood stream. I did a project on cobras at school," Rani said. "See the yellow serum coming from the fangs into the dish."

Shivers rippled up Ben's entire body. "Do the men ever get bitten?"

"Sometimes, but watch how calm and slow their movements are. They are followers of the god Shiva, who protects them from snake bites."

Ben remembered that Shiva was the father of Ganesh. He also protected people from snake bites? What next?

Ben took some photographs and caught a good one of the men carrying the snake back to the rocks after they'd finished the milking. As the snake was released, the men stepped back quickly and the snake slithered into a hole under the rocks.

"My grandmother and I saw snake charmers in Delhi, at

the Red Fort. They looked dangerous," Ben said. "My grand-mother spazzed."

Rani laughed. "Oh, those snakes are harmless. I see them often in shows and they've had their poison sacs removed. When they strike out at the crowd, it's effective for the shows, but it's just a trick to make money."

"That's wicked!"

Rani went on. "I'll tell you something else. People don't know it, but cobras are deaf, so the music the snake charmers play on their flutes is just for dramatic effect."

"Worked on me!" said Ben.

Ben stood in the clearing beside Rani. The sun was warm on his back, the scratchy-voiced parrots kept up their rau-cous calls, monkeys howled from high in the trees, and near-by two incandescent blue and orange butterflies chased each other in a flashing dance.

None of it felt real to Ben. Here he was, Benjamin Leeson from Vancouver, standing in the jungle beside an Indian girl, a metre away from men milking a poisonous snake! Some-how, the things you saw in India filled your head and didn't leave space for anything else.

Rani interrupted Ben's trance. "It's after four o'clock, Ben. We'd better get back to your grandmother."

He hadn't given Gran a thought for hours. "You're right. We have to go."

Ben ran for his bike, Rani followed and they wheeled onto the path. Ben began to cycle furiously, glancing behind to be sure Rani was following. How could he be so selfish? He was the only person Gran knew in India and he'd said he'd be back at four. Now it was over twenty-four hours since he'd seen her. She could have started vomiting again. Or worse.

Bumping over ruts in the road and sliding too fast around corners, Ben heard Rani call out behind him. He braked and turned around. Rani had crashed her bike and was lying on the rough gravel road.

Ben dropped his bike and ran back, but as he reached her, Rani sat up and looked at Ben with startled eyes. There was dirt on her blouse and along the skin of her arm. She held her arm with her other hand, and her face was twisted in pain.

This was his fault. He'd rushed away in a panic, thinking that Gran might be dead, and poor Rani had been trying to keep up. His fault.

"Please help me stand, Ben." Rani's voice was unsteady. "Take my other arm."

Once on her feet, Rani tried to brush the dirt off her blouse, but Ben could see it hurt too much. Not until she gave him a weak smile could Ben allow himself to speak. "I'm sorry. It's my fault. I made you rush."

"I wasn't watching and I hit a dip in the road back there. I'm okay, Ben."

"Your arm is hurt," Ben stammered.

"Not badly. Let's keep going to the hospital. The out-patient infirmary will take care of it. You should get to your grandmother. Come on, Ben."

Ben picked up her bike. At least it was still working. Ben

wheeled both bikes beside Rani as she set the pace for a quick trip to the hospital. Rani still used her left hand to support her right arm. She was pale; her arm was probably broken. Ben's watch said it was almost five. He didn't know who to worry about the most — his grandmother or Rani. But he knew who was to blame for everything.

He led Rani to the hospital infirmary, where a nurse told her to take a seat. Rani waved him away. "Leave me here, Ben. Go to your grandmother."

"Okay," Ben said, gratefully. "But I'll come back as soon as I can."

At the end of the long room Gran was sitting up in the hospital bed, eating from food on a tray. Her face looked normal, not the grey colour it had been the day before, but when she saw Ben her lips began to tremble. "Where have you been?"

"Oh, Gran. I'm sorry I'm so late. I forgot about the time and then —"

"Ben. I've been worried that something had happened to you." She started to cry; when she tried to wipe her eyes with the hospital gown, she knocked over a bowl on the tray.

"All night and all day with only the nurses to talk to." She was making a mess of wiping up the soup and sobbed even harder. "I saw you drowning. Or hit by a truck. And I wasn't there to help you. I'm responsible for you and I was stuck here."

Ben took the tray and put it on the side table. He put his

hand on his grandmother's arm. "I'm sorry. Really sorry. But you shouldn't have worried. I was fine. Rani took me to watch cobras being milked —"

"You were watching *cobras* being milked? Oh, heavens, it scares me out of my mind to hear you say that!" There was soup all over her hospital gown and tears dripping down her face.

Ben moved closer. "It was so interesting. The snakes were so huge —"

"Don't say another word!" Her face was getting red and she was waving her arms wildly in the air.

A nurse appeared at the bed and leaned over to Gran. "What happened, Mrs. Leeson?"

He heard Gran say something and the nurse pulled the curtain, shutting him out. Ben stood limply outside the curtain. When would he learn? He shouldn't have mentioned snakes.

The nurse hurried away and came back with a cold cloth and a glass of water. Ben waited until she left, and Gran called to him.

Her face was puffy. "Sorry for the outburst, Ben. I'm ashamed I made such a fuss. I've just been so worried about you and then to find out you've been with cobras —" She pointed to the chair beside her bed and Ben sat down.

Now it was his turn. Ben could feel the tears pushing against his eyes. Don't cry, he told himself. It had all been too much: worrying about being late, then Rani's accident and now being yelled at. Gran handed him a tissue.

"Don't be upset, Ben. They've taken good care of me here. Dr. Dhaliwal is wonderful. He's coming by this afternoon to unhook me from this contraption." She pointed to the needle in her hand. "If all's well, he says I can go back to our bungalow tonight."

She patted his arm. "How's Rani?"

"She's in the infirmary."

"What's the matter?" Gran said, alarmed.

"A bike accident on our way here. I was rushing to see you and she crashed her bike. I'm worried her arm is broken."

"Oh, my heavens. Poor Rani."

Just then Dr. Dhaliwal arrived. "Your grandmother's done well, Ben. You can pick her up tonight at seven, but she'll need to rest the next few days."

"Thanks. It's a great hospital you've got here, Dr. Dhaliwal."

"We're proud of our Indian hospitals," said the doctor. "Please come with me, Ben, to get medicine for your grandmother."

Ben told Gran he'd be back before seven and waited outside the pharmacy until Dr. Dhaliwal came back with some pills. "These will balance your grandmother's system and get her back to normal."

Ben took the pills. This was his chance. "Dr. Dhaliwal, do you remember you told me that you went to medical school with a man called Dr. Mukherjee? We heard that Shanti's brother went to medical school."

"Could be the same man. He was a nice fellow. Let me look him up in the medical registry to see if I have an address for you."

"That would be great," Ben said.

"My advice is not to tell your grandmother about this yet. She doesn't need another disappointment while she's getting her strength back."

"I agree. I already scared her talking about snakes," Ben said. "I hope you find the man's address. It could be a good lead, Dr. Dhaliwal." Ben didn't say it but there weren't any other leads. If this one failed, the game would be over. No camel hair in the desert. No pen pal.

Dr. Dhaliwal turned to go. "I'll let you know when I come by the resort tomorrow."

The nurse in the infirmary had just finished wrapping Rani's wrist in an elastic bandage. Rani smiled at him. "It's just a sprain, Ben. Don't be so alarmed."

The nurse helped her up. "You'll be fine in a few days, young lady. Take it easy on that bike."

"Does it hurt?" Ben asked Rani on the way out of the hospital.

"A little bit."

"I wish I hadn't made you rush."

"Now you'll have to help with my morning chores," Rani laughed, and Ben knew she was all right.

Rani was able to push her bike beside him through town.

She stopped at a statue of Ganesh outside a small temple. Ben saw that again, the elephant's large head was festooned with a ring of marigolds. There was a bowl of candy at his feet.

"I wanted to show you this. See how children put sweets beside Ganesh? They're asking him to help with a problem."

"Let's try it," Ben said.

On their way to the shop, Ben realized that Rani hadn't mentioned the fanny pack and thought he should explain. He pointed at it. "I know this makes me look geeky, but I promised my grandmother I'd take care of our money."

Rani nodded. "Oh, the money belt. Lots of people wear one."

"You've seen teenage boys wearing a pack like this?" Ben asked.

"All the time. Makes good sense."

Well, if he could call it a money belt, maybe it wasn't so bad. Ben pulled the wallet out of his pocket. "Think I should use my own money to buy the sweets." He bought lemon candy for Ganesh and roasted cashew nuts for his grand-mother.

After he'd placed the candy at Ganesh's feet, Ben looked into the statue's eyes and sent a silent message: You helped me find a way out of the temple, Ganesh. Please help me again. Let Dr. Dhaliwal find an address for Shanti's brother.

To Rani he said out loud, "We're running out of time. I sure hope this stuff about Ganesh works."

Dear Mum and Lauren

Gran will be home tonight. She spazzed when I told her
I saw cobras being milked. Now I've got Ganesh, the
elephant god, helping me 2 find Shanti.

Good luck in the semis, Lauren.

Ben

By eight o'clock, Gran was back in the bungalow and tucked up in bed with a bowl of cashew nuts on the table beside her, and the room filled with the peppery-sweet smell of the yellow jasmine that Mrs. Gurin had placed in the room.

"I'll be fine here. I just want to sleep," Gran said. "Why don't you go and see how Rani's feeling?"

"I won't be late," Ben said. He knocked on the Gurin's door and asked Rani if she felt well enough for another game of chess.

"I'm there," she said, and they both laughed. "But if I lose, I'll have my injury as an excuse!"

Chess was a bit like computer battles. You moved the players around and tried to knock out your opponents. After an hour, Ben paused, thought for a long moment, then moved his rook to threaten Rani's king. "Check," he said, trying to hold back a smile. Rani studied the board and looked up at Ben.

"Mate," said Ben. "Checkmate!"

"Quick learner," Rani said.

"Good teacher," Ben answered.

As Ben returned to his bungalow, the familiar pounding of the breaking waves rolled across the grass toward him. Rani would be okay and his grandmother was well again. For the first time in a long time, all seemed right with the world.

Days Ten, Eleven and Twelve

"THE RESORT WILL SOON be filled with tourists," Rani said. "Our busy season is coming up."

Ben put the last folded towel on top of the pile. Even with her sprained wrist Rani's pile was neater, but he'd seen her wince again when she started to lift the towels. "Let me carry those," he said as he followed her out of the laundry room. "Does your wrist hurt much today?"

"It hurt last night, but it's better now."

"You and Prem sure help your mother a lot, Rani."

"Oh, yes," Rani said. "It would be too much for her to manage the resort alone. Prem does the office work, and I help the two women from the village when I'm on school holidays."

Ben thought of his mother in their kitchen at home in Vancouver. He could see her rushing to put in laundry and empty the dishwasher, her ponytail flipping out behind her. And this was after she'd had a full day at the office. Ben felt ashamed. When she'd asked for help, he hadn't done much. Being here and watching Rani had made him think. Ben made himself a promise: he would load and unload the dishwasher every day when he got home. And he'd do it without being asked.

Rani interrupted Ben's thoughts. "I'd like to take you to see something special when we finish here. That is, if you want to."

"What is it?" Ben asked as he finished piling the towels in the storage cupboard.

"There's an interesting cave up the beach."

"A cave. Epic!"

Rani led the way past rolling sand dunes and along the hard sand. About a kilometre up the beach they arrived at a small stone cave close to the water's edge.

"The cave floods at high tide," Rani said. "Low tide is the only time to see the carvings inside."

Ben followed her down wet stone steps into the shadowy cave. The smell of rotting seaweed crept up from the clammy floor, and the dank air made his head feel thick. The only light in the cave came down in a narrow shaft from a hole in the roof. Ben waited for his eyes to adjust. Slowly, he began to see that three large elephants had been carved around the walls. He traced the rough trunk of the first elephant with his hand. He noticed the elephant's front leg was raised, bent at the knee. Underneath the raised foot, something else had been carved. The crouching figure with its back exposed was hard to see in the half-light. It looked like a child. Surely the carver hadn't meant to show the elephant about to crush a child.

Ben turned to ask Rani and realized they'd become separated. The cave was so dark he couldn't see across it. He called, "Rani?"

Rani . . . Rani . . . Rani. His call echoed around the damp walls and back to meet him. He called again, "Are you there, Rani?"

Then, out of the dim light, she came up beside him. "I'm here, Ben."

"I couldn't see you."

"I know, we were together at the entrance and then you were gone."

"There's something strange about this carving. See under the elephant's raised foot? It's hard to see properly, but I think it's a child."

Rani bent down beside Ben. "It *is* a child. See the small face hidden by the hand?"

"He seems alone." Somehow Ben knew it was a boy.

"No one has been able to understand the drawings in this cave. Look at the next carving," Rani said. "The child is sitting in the curve of the elephant's trunk."

Ben thought that looked like fun. He moved along to the

last carving. "Now the boy is on the elephant's back."

Rani nodded. "Elephants do use their trunks to lift people onto their backs."

"The boy's different up there. Excited. Happy."

"I see that too," Rani said.

"I think these carvings are telling a story," Ben said. But what was it? Someone had found this cave and come back with a chisel to carve the boy and the elephants. The carvings were hundreds of years old; they had nothing to do with him. Why did seeing them make him feel so uncomfortable?

On the way back, Ben was lost in his own thoughts. Rani was quiet too until they reached the top of the sand dunes when she said, "Let me show you something special," and led him along the cliff where they could get closer to the lighthouse.

"A priest lives there," she said. "Sometimes people see two eagles circling over the lighthouse. It is said the eagles come all the way from Varanasi. If you are lucky enough to see the eagles coming down to take the food the priest puts out for them, you are promised good fortune."

"Have you seen them?" asked Ben.

Rani smiled. "I'll tell you a strange thing. I always come up here to look for them, but never had I seen them until last week. It was just before you and your grandmother arrived that I saw them for the first time. They were magnificent." Rani looked down. "Perhaps your arrival was good fortune for me."

"And me," said Ben. He could feel himself blushing.

At the resort, Gran was dressed and strolling in the garden with Rani's mother.

"You must be better, Gran!" Ben said. He told her about the elephant caves, but not, for some reason, about the small boy. And he didn't tell her about the eagles who were known to appear at the lighthouse.

That afternoon, Dr. Dhaliwal came by and pronounced Gran well. Ben waited to talk to the doctor alone and went with him to his car. "Dr. Dhaliwal, did you find out about Shanti's brother?"

"Yes, Ben. I did locate him." He handed Ben a piece of paper from his pocket. "I suggest you try contacting my old student friend by email. There's a possibility that Dr. Vivek Mukherjee is Shanti's brother. Please say hello from me."

At last, a real lead for finding Shanti. As the doctor opened his car door, Ben said, "Thanks, and thanks for taking such good care of my grandmother."

"You are most welcome, Ben. I like your grandmother."

Ben looked at the doctor's kind face. "I've never met a Sikh before. Rani told me you wear a turban because you're a Sikh."

"Indeed, it is our tradition to grow our hair long and to keep it covered. Here, you see, we also wear this bracelet called a *kara*." He pulled up his shirt cuff to show Ben the metal bracelet on his wrist.

"Do Sikhs believe in reincarnation?"

"Indeed, like Hindus, we believe in the immortality of the soul. We believe souls have many lives."

"I've been thinking a lot about death. I mean, since my dad died. I just have a hard time understanding how the souls of dead people can come back to earth." Ben wondered why he was talking so much to a man he hardly knew.

"I'm sorry about your father, Ben. What happens after death is a big question and it is good that you are thinking about it." He got into the car, leaned out the window and ran his hand through his long beard. "Perhaps you will find the answer here in India."

"Thanks, Dr. Dhaliwal." Ben said. He looked at the paper and rushed to find Rani.

In the office, they quickly keyed in the doctor's email address. Leaning over the keyboard, Rani helped Ben compose a message.

Dear Dr. Vivek Mukherjee

I am a Canadian in India with my grandmother who would like to contact a pen pal she had in the 1940s. The pen pal's name was Shanti Mukherjee and she went to the Calcutta Senior Girls' School. Are you related to her? Dr. Dhaliwal here in Mahabalipuram gave me your address and says to say hello.

Thank you for your help.

Ben Leeson

c/o pgurin@interweb.com

"I'll check the school site once more," Ben said.

"Last chance," Rani said.

The site came up, but there were no messages about Shanti. Ben clicked off the computer and stared at the blank screen. How many times had he rushed to the computer, sure that someone would be contacting him about Shanti? He was sick of hoping.

"It's time to give up on that idea," Rani said. "I'm sure Dr. Mukherjee will answer your email."

"Ganesh had better hurry up and make it happen. We've only got six more days in India."

Ben and Rani went swimming every day, and Gran took longer and longer walks around the garden. Sitting on the veranda at either side of a small wicker table, Gran and Ben were having lunch made by Rani and her mother. Ben looked across at his grandmother. She was different since she'd been sick. She never mentioned Shanti, and she seemed to have forgotten all about finding her. Now, he was the one who was obsessed with the search.

Maybe he should tell her he'd emailed Dr. Mukherjee, but there was a chance the doctor might not be Shanti's brother, and he didn't want to get Gran's hopes up. Besides it would be cool to surprise her.

Gran's appetite was back and she looked like she was enjoying the lunch of rice and dhal. "I'm glad you're feeling better, Gran. I was scared you were going to die."

"For a few hours there I wouldn't have minded!" she laughed. "But thanks to you, Ben, I got the help I needed."

Gran was thanking *him* for helping her. He was the grandson who'd abandoned her in the hospital and then scared her so much by talking about cobras.

Gran put down her glass of lemonade. "I'm sorry I panicked when you told me about the snakes. It's an irrational fear that I'm not proud of."

"I feel awful that I was late coming to see you in the hospital. I got so involved in what we were seeing, I forgot about the time." That didn't sound very good. "I don't mean I forgot about you, Gran."

"I know what you mean, Ben," Gran said. "It was so hard being stuck in that hospital bed, thinking something might have happened to you. I feel responsible for you here in India."

"We're responsible for each other, Gran."

"I'm proud of you, Ben. How you took care of yourself when I was in the hospital." Gran finished the meal and smiled at him.

She had the same strong face as his father. "My dad worried about me too. You and Dad are a lot alike."

"You make me think of your dad, Ben."

Ben shifted in his seat. "I wish I hadn't been so mean, blaming you for his smoking. It wasn't your fault."

Gran nodded her head. "When something sad happens we'd all like to have someone to blame."

Now seemed like a good time. "I have something for you, Gran." He went to a drawer in his room and came back with the baseball cap that said DELHI DEVILS. He'd decided not to confess that he'd left her hat behind in the taxi. It wasn't exactly lying, and he *had* bought her a new one.

"Well, well. Thank you. I looked for my hat, but I couldn't find it. This will do nicely." She tried it on and admired herself in the mirror. Ben had to admit that, for an old lady, she looked good.

That afternoon, after playing chess with Rani, Ben checked the computer again. His heart was beating fast as he logged in, but there was no message from Dr. Mukherjee. He'd been right not to mention anything to Gran.

There was a message from Lauren and his mother. They were relieved that Gran was doing well, and they were busy shovelling more snow.

When Ben got out of bed the following morning, there was no sign of Gran in their bungalow. He dressed and searched for her over by the Gurins' bungalow. Rani hadn't seen Gran either, but by the time they'd looked all over the grounds, Gran was coming up from the beach toward them.

Her face was glowing. "I went for an early morning walk to the lighthouse and saw the most interesting thing."

"Tell us," Rani and Ben said together.

"There were two white-headed eagles circling the tower. Huge ones like our bald eagles, Ben." She stopped to catch her breath. "The priest came out and put food on a rock for them. They swooped right down and grabbed the food. I've never seen eagles so close!"

Rani was almost jumping up and down. "Oh, Mrs. Leeson,

that means you will have good fortune!"

"I wish." Gran's smile faded. "I'm afraid the good fortune I need most in India is not going to happen."

"But it will, Mrs. Leeson," Rani said. "Now that you have seen the eagles at the lighthouse, it will."

"I'm afraid we're out of time. Our trip is almost over." Gran sighed.

"Did you check for an email this morning?" Rani whispered to Ben.

"Yep."

"Any luck?"

"Nope."

That afternoon, they went in Prem's car to see a famous temple not far from town. "Such a handsome hat, Mrs. Leeson," Mrs. Gurin said.

"Ben chose it for me," Gran answered.

The massive grey stone temple sat in the middle of a field of grass. Ben and Gran were amazed to see the outside was completely covered in carvings. A group of schoolgirls in white blouses and navy skirts sat cross-legged in front of it, drawing the figures while their teachers wandered among them, their bright saris blowing in the wind.

"The carvings on this temple are very old," Prem explained. "They show a Hindu legend that tells us that all gods, animals and humans sprang from the source of the Ganges River."

The carvings were of men and women harvesting and winnowing rice, washing clothes, cooking on open fires and playing with their children.

"Look at the tigers and elephants!" said Gran.

"All the Hindu gods are there too," said Mrs. Gurin.

"Ben, there's Ganesh!" Rani pointed to a carving of the elephant god high on the temple. "See, on either side are his parents, Shiva and Parvati."

"Poor Shiva chopping off his son's head by mistake," Prem said.

"Yes, but now we have a boy god especially to help children," Rani said.

"I'm waiting . . . ," Ben said, winking at her.

Gran and Mrs. Gurin were resting on a grassy knoll when the others joined them. They watched the schoolchildren and their teachers pack up their drawings and leave in a van.

"Reminds me that I'll be back at school next week," said Rani.

"And I'll be on my way back to Canada," Ben said.

It was three days since Gran had come out of the hospital. The time was going too fast, and still no Shanti.

As soon as they returned Ben and Rani rushed to the computer. There was one message.

Greetings to Mr. Ben Leeson

I have been away for two days so did not receive your message until this morning. I believe that the Shanti Mukherjee you seek is indeed my sister who

did write to a Canadian pen pal many years ago. Shanti
is widowed now and presently lives with her daughter's
family in Rishikesh. She has two grandsons. There is
something your grandmother must know before she
meets Shanti. It would be best if you come first to
Bangalore so I can explain. It is on the way to Rishikesh.

With good wishes

Dr. Vivek Mukherjee

Gran sat up as she saw the two of them running across the
grass to the veranda.

"Gran! Gran! The eagles brought you good luck," Ben
called. "We've just had an email from Dr. Mukherjee, Shanti's
brother." He stopped to catch his breath. "We've found Shanti
and she has grandchildren, just like you!"

Gran gasped. "Shanti is alive. I can't believe it." She stood
up and did a little dance. "Is it really true?"

Ben laughed. "She lives in the north, in Rishikesh, Gran."

Giggling at Gran's dance, Rani said, "It is a famous place
close to the source of the Ganges River."

Gran turned to Rani. "You don't mean the place that was
represented in the cave carvings today?"

"Yes," said Rani. "It is amazing that we should have been
to that temple today!"

"I can't believe any of this." Gran said, sitting down. "After
all these years. To think I've finally found Shanti."

"Her brother wants to see us first to explain something,"
Ben said.

"What could he have to explain?" Gran said. "You don't think Shanti is dying, do you?"

Oh, no . . . not more dying. Ben turned away.

Gran didn't look happy anymore. "I couldn't bear it. To come all this way. . ." She shook her head. "No, I think I know what it is. Shanti's brother knows she's angry with me. He'll tell me she refuses to see me."

"I don't think it could be that, Mrs. Leeson," Rani said.

"Whatever it is, I have to know." Gran had that determined look again. "Please email Dr. Mukherjee to tell him we're coming, Ben."

Within an hour a reply came from Dr. Mukherjee, giving them the address of his clinic in the centre of Bangalore. Prem agreed to make arrangements for them to leave early the next morning for the six-hour bus ride. Gran went to invite the Gurins for a farewell dinner in town that night. In a few hours, Ben would have to say goodbye to Rani.

Ben and Gran were waiting outside when Mrs. Gurin and Rani came across the lawn dressed in long saris.

"Oh, how lovely!" Gran said. "I feel very plain in my travelling clothes."

It was the first time Ben had seen Rani in anything other than western clothes. Her light pink sari had a border of deeper pink trimmed with silver that curved over her shoulders. Her hair was loose, and glistened in the evening light. Coloured glass bracelets jangled up one arm. An elastic bandage was wrapped around her other arm. She smiled at Ben's face as he stared at her long gold earrings and diamond nose pin.

Following the others, Ben walked beside Rani on the way to town. At the side of the path, blossoming parajit trees flooded the warm night air with a honey-sweet smell. Not for the first time in India, Ben felt as though he were part of a movie set.

Prem had reserved a private room in the restaurant, and they sat around a table spread with a white cloth.

"You might like to try some goat curry," Rani teased Ben.

"I forbid anyone to eat goat curry tonight!" Ben answered.

Rani batted her dark eyelashes, showing the black kohl around her eyes. She put her hand on her heart. "My Canadian hero," she sighed.

The table was loaded as the waiter brought dish after dish of rice, breads and vegetable curries. For a moment things were quiet, then Gran spoke up. "I'd like to ask you something that's been on my mind, Rani. You're the young woman here. Tell me what you think about arranged marriages."

Ben squirmed in his seat. This was embarrassing. Why would Gran question Rani about this right now? At their last dinner together.

The question didn't seem to bother Rani, who answered right away. "The girls at school all feel that because we'll go to university and work out in the world, we'll most probably meet our future husband ourselves. We will know if we are attracted to someone."

Were her cheeks a little flushed?

Prem added. "I feel the same way, Mrs. Leeson. Though of course, we have great respect for our elders and want them to be part of our decision."

"Yes," said Rani. "I would certainly want approval from my mother and Prem. They know me best and want me to marry the right person."

Gran was thoughtful. "Things have changed then, from the way it was for the older generation of Indian women?"

"Oh, yes," said Mrs. Gurin. "My dear husband was chosen for me. I saw him for the first time on my wedding day." She smiled at Gran. "Of course, I grew to love him very much. My parents had chosen wisely for me."

"Things are different now," Prem said. "It used to be that a dowry was required of the wife's family. Now the giving of dowries is against the law, but still it is a custom for families to give money, sometimes even a cow, to the prospective husband."

"You mean you get a cow when you choose a wife?" Ben asked.

"Cows are valuable, you see," Prem said.

"Not nearly as valuable as a good wife!" Rani said, making everyone laugh. "I'm glad compulsory dowries are against the law now."

Gran beamed around the table at everyone. "Thanks to our friends, the Gurin family, for giving us so much help and being such good company. You will always have a special place in my heart."

Mine too, thought Ben.

On the way back to the resort, Rani said to Ben, "Now can you understand how seeing the eagles brought good fortune to your grandmother?"

"I think Ganesh had a hand — maybe a trunk — in it too, don't you? All those lemon sweets I gave him!" Ben said.

"I'm happy for your grandmother, but sad you're leaving so soon."

"I'll come back to India one day. I promise you that. And you won't need eagles to tell you when." Ben moved his fingers over an imaginary keyboard. "I'll be sending an email!"

When they returned to the compound, Ben asked Rani to wait while he got something from his room.

"This is to help you remember me." Ben put his red baseball cap that said CANADA on Rani's head. She looked so awesome that his heart gave a thump. He almost reached out to take her hand, but stopped himself. All of a sudden Ben felt shy. "Like it?" he asked.

"Yep," answered Rani with a toss of her dark hair.

Day Thirteen

AS THE DRIVER RELEASED the air brakes and backed the bus out of the terminal, Ben had a last glimpse of Rani. She wore the baseball cap and she was waving at him. Waving with her bandaged arm. That meant it was better.

Sitting in the front seat, Ben turned and looked back at the other passengers on the bus. He and Gran were the only foreigners. He had the window seat and struggled to open the window to get rid of the stuffy air, but it wouldn't move. Gran was kicking aside the peanut shells and plastic wrap under her feet. Then the driver flicked a switch, sending a blast of Bollywood music out of the speakers above their heads.

The bus lurched onto the highway and soon they were passing through fields of tall green sugar cane. At the side of the road, two white bullocks with long curved horns pulled a cart loaded with cane stalks. A local bus careened past them on the narrow road, with passengers packed inside and piles of luggage teetering on the overloaded rooftop. Farther along, women in saris marched at the side of the road, balancing stones on their heads, delivering them to workmen who were repairing the road.

Inside the bus, the raucous movie music blared; passengers smoked and talked incessantly, babies cried, the air got heavier. Ben wrote Rani's name in the dust on the window. Suddenly, Gran leaned over him, shouting to be heard above the music. "See across from us, one row back — that man with the woven basket beside him? I've been watching. The basket is moving!"

Ben leaned across Gran to look. Not only was the basket shifting on the seat, but something inside was pushing against the lid and the only thing that kept it from opening were two handles crossed over the top. As Ben watched, the basket gave a violent jerk.

"It's a snake!" Gran was on her feet. She was shouting. "I know it! It's a live snake!" She scrambled across Ben to get to the window seat as far away from the aisle as possible. She put her face in her hands and her shoulders rocked from side to side. Muffled whimpering sounds came from behind her hands. Ben hoped she wouldn't scream again.

Gran lowered her shaking hands and turned to him. "This is my worst nightmare come true. There's a poisonous snake right beside us in this bus. *Get it away, Ben!*"

Ben tried to tell her what he knew about performing cobras. "It's okay, Gran. Rani said snake charmers take the poison sacs out of their snakes. They're completely harmless."

"I don't *care!*" She poked his arm. "Poison sacs or not, there's still a live snake inside that basket and the stupid man hasn't even tied the lid on! *I can't stand it. Do something. Please!*"

Sure enough, a narrow flute rested beside the man. It was a snake charmer with his snake all right, almost certainly a cobra, and those straw handles were quite flimsy. He stared at the man who had his eyes closed and seemed to be sleeping.

Maybe Rani had been wrong. Maybe snakes out here in the country were not the same as big city snakes. Whatever the truth was, he and his grandmother were inside a bus tearing down the highway with a live cobra across the aisle.

Ben jumped when Gran shook his shoulder and yelled in his ear. "Ben, tell the driver to make that man take the snake off the bus! Why would they let a snake get on a bus anyway? *Go on, tell him!*" Her whole body was trembling.

Ben tried to reason with her. "Snake charmers have a right to be on a bus. They have to travel, just like us." He saw that the man had woken, probably from Gran's yelling. "Gran, he's got his hand on the lid. The snake can't get out now."

It was as though she hadn't heard him. *"We're trapped!"* shrieked Gran. She was gasping for air in an alarming way.

Was this how someone behaved when they were having a panic attack? Weren't you supposed to throw water on their faces? No point looking in his pack. He didn't have any water.

Just then, the bus slowed and the driver pulled into an open area with a few huts. It was obviously a stop for food, and Gran became desperate to get out. She leapt over Ben, caught her foot on his shin and sprawled, face across his lap. Her skirt had twisted around her legs, and her arms thrashed wildly in the aisle, perilously close to the man with the snake. Uttering shrill yaps that reminded Ben of an angry Pekingese, his grandmother scrambled to get on her feet. Attempting to push down her skirt, she stumbled and shoved her way past the other passengers to get out of the bus.

Ben slid down in his seat; the other passengers filed off, followed by the snake charmer, his flute in one hand and the basket in the other. Ben bent down to pick up his grandmother's baseball cap, hooked his backpack over his shoulder and was the last off the bus.

His grandmother was sitting hunched over on a bench in the dirt square. He went closer; her hands were pressed into her face, but the Pekingese noises had stopped.

"Here's your hat, Gran," he said, dusting it off and sitting down beside her. "You'll be fine now. See, the snake charmer is way up the road. He probably lives near here."

Gran took a deep breath and wiped her face. Gradually she stopped shaking, but her face was puffy and her grey hair stuck up in all directions, making her look as though she'd been in a windstorm. Her voice was raspy and tight. "Just let me get myself together, Ben."

Ben went to one of the stalls and brought back the only drink he could find — a red syrupy drink in a plastic bag, with a straw sticking through the hole where the bag had been tied. It was good to be in charge of the money and he'd never admit it to Gran, but he liked carrying their rupees in the money belt. They felt safe there.

Ben noticed some bus passengers standing in a circle to watch a show. He told Gran he wanted to see what it was and made his way to the front. A tall performer was holding up a box of metal nails. One by one the man began swallowing the nails; large ones, small ones, whole clusters of nails were disappearing down his throat. The man dipped his chin and swallowed over and over again.

Then, signalling the crowd to pay attention, he began to cough up the nails, singly and in clumps, spitting them into the tin box. If Ben wasn't standing right in front of the man, he never would have believed it. The man rubbed his throat, bowed and passed around a cup for the crowd to show their gratitude. Along with everyone else, Ben dropped in coins from his pocket.

"You should have seen that guy, Gran," Ben said, sitting down beside her. "It was amazing." He passed Gran one of the samosas the Gurins had sent with them.

"I just can't eat," she said. "I'm sorry for my outburst, Ben. I've never actually been that close to a live snake."

"No problem now, Gran. The guy and his snake are way gone."

"I feel ashamed of myself. I'm just going to sit quietly until the bus leaves."

Ben turned and saw a young boy half-lying on a skateboard rolling toward him. The boy had no legs and his body ended where his legs should have started. Ben stared. The boy was about eight or nine and had a grim set to his lean face. Using his arms, he was propelling himself through the dirt, coming closer and calling for rupees. How could anyone live like that? To have to lie on a skateboard and beg because you had no legs.

The passengers waiting to get back on the bus saw the boy, but only a few tossed coins to him. Ben opened his backpack and took out the last two bananas and put them on the skateboard. He hesitated a moment, then reached for his pocket knife and put it in the boy's hand. The boy stared up at Ben, then back down at the knife. Ben nodded to show the boy he could keep the knife and was rewarded with a smile that lit up the boy's entire face.

Ben crouched down beside the skateboard to demonstrate the three blades, the scissors and the bottle opener. He watched while the boy tested the longest blade for sharpness against his finger. They were both so absorbed that Ben didn't hear the bus doors close and the driver start the engine. He didn't notice the bus swing out of the clearing until the back wheels sent dust spitting down on the two of them. He stood up to see the bus tearing down the road. Gran had let the driver leave without him!

Ben grabbed his backpack and began to run down the highway. He ran as fast as he could, panting hard, breathing in dust, until he realized he'd never catch the bus. He slowed, staggered and after a while, stopped.

He tried to get his thoughts together. Here he was, thirteen years old, alone on a dusty road somewhere in south India. Too old to cry. Too scared to hitch a ride. Too stupid to have any other ideas about what to do.

Ben watched the bus get smaller and smaller, his thoughts whirling. He hadn't wanted to be on the stupid bus anyway. What he really wanted was to be back on the beach with Rani.

Then, like something seen from the wrong end of a pair of binoculars, the bus stopped, turned and headed back along the road toward him.

The passengers cheered when Ben climbed on — everyone but Gran, whose face was as white as a snowman's. He thumped himself down beside her.

"I'm so sorry, Ben." She spoke quickly, sounding like a kid who's had a bad scare. "When I got on I had to check to make sure the snake wasn't anywhere on the bus, and I was so tired, I just sat down and closed my eyes. When I looked

over and saw you weren't beside me, I panicked." Her eyes
pleaded with Ben to understand. "I rushed up to the driver
as fast as I could but it was hard to make him understand
we'd left you behind. He didn't speak English so I was using
sign language, pointing to your seat, holding up two fingers,
doing everything I could to get him to turn around."

Another time Ben might have laughed at the thought of
his grandmother using sign language with the bus driver,
but not now. "I just can't believe you let the bus drive away
without me! I stood there on the road thinking I'd never
find you. I thought I'd have to get back to Canada by myself."

"I'm sorry, very sorry." Gran's face was crumbling.

Ben wiped his sweaty forehead and reached in his pack
for water. The grit in his teeth reminded him of the mouthful of dirt he'd eaten on a dare when he was four. Of course,
there was no water in his pack.

"This trip has been one disaster after another. I'm sick of
it. I wish I was back in Canada right now," he said.

"I don't blame you, Ben. I feel angry with myself. I talk to
you about being responsible and then I do a thing like this.
I wish the trip was over too."

Ben didn't like to hear his grandmother say that. It was
okay if a kid said it; you blurt out all kinds of things when
you're fuming mad at being dumped on the side of the road.
"You don't mean that, Gran."

"I guess not, but we have no idea why Shanti's brother

asked to see us. I'm worried about what we're going to find out."

Ben was too, but there was no point trying to guess what it was. He leaned back on the seat.

"What were you doing back there, anyway, Ben? Didn't you see everyone getting on the bus?"

"I gave my pocket knife to that boy without legs and I was showing him some of the neat things about it."

"You let him have the pocket knife I gave you for Christmas?"

"I'm sorry, Gran. I had to. That boy had nothing."

"But you used that knife all the time to peel fruit."

"I loved that knife, and I'll miss it. Remember I used the scissors to make cut-offs out of these jeans?"

"I'm surprised you'd give it away."

"I gave it to him without thinking, but I'm glad I did. That boy was the most handicapped person I've ever seen. He has a terrible life ahead of him. I can get another knife, but that boy won't ever get anything special."

Gran smiled at him. "I think I understand, Ben."

Gran was quiet, and Ben's thoughts were about the boy. Ben wondered how he'd lost both legs. Could he have been born like that? Or been in some kind of horrible accident? He'd never forget the boy's smile when he'd realized he could keep the knife.

The rocking of the bus calmed Ben, and his eyes closed. He and Gran would be in Canada in a few days. Maybe they'd leave on the plane without ever seeing Shanti. He'd been so certain he'd find her on the site of her old school; he'd imagined Gran admiring him, saying how smart he was. She'd say the computer did have some useful things about it, after all. But now, unexpectedly, just because Gran had been sick, they'd met Dr. Dhaliwal and were on their way to meet Shanti's brother. It was funny how things worked. If she hadn't got sick, they'd be back to where they were the day they'd arrived in India. Now they might be close to actually meeting Shanti. Maybe it would all work out, but then, being India, it just as likely might not. Ben could feel himself dozing off.

He opened his eyes and realized the bus was passing small shacks and houses that were probably the outskirts of Bangalore. They passed more shops on suburban streets and finally came to a halt at the city bus terminal. It was four o'clock in the afternoon when they got off the bus.

"Let's find a hotel and go to see Dr. Mukherjee while his clinic is still open," Gran said. Her sleep on the bus seemed to have helped her recover, both from the scare with the cobra and from leaving him behind on the road.

A bicycle rickshaw driver took them to the Hotel Paradise. "It is owned by a friend of my very good friend. Most comfortable hotel in all Bangalore," he said. "You will be thanking me."

Gran was pleased that the hotel was both reasonably priced and pleasant, with an attractive interior courtyard that backed onto a dining room. A porter took their back-packs to a shady room on the second floor with two single beds, a desk and a small bathroom.

The rickshaw driver was leaning against his bicycle wait-ing for them when they came back down.

"Could we stop on the way so I can buy a new cap?" Ben said.

"What happened to your red Canada one?" Gran asked.

"Rani liked it so I gave it to her."

"Hmm," was all Gran said. Exactly the same reaction he'd expect from his mother when she didn't want to make a comment.

They stopped at a stall and Ben found another red cap, this one with MUMBAI MINIS written over the brim.

"Whatever they are," he said to Gran.

Wearing their baseball caps, the two of them perched like royalty on the high rickshaw seat on the way to Dr. Mukher-jee's clinic.

As they walked up to the large bungalow that housed the clinic, a dapper man with wire frame glasses like the kind Gandhi wore and a short white coat came toward them, his hand outstretched.

"Welcome. Welcome. Welcome Mrs. Leeson and welcome Mr. Ben. I am your servant Dr. Vivek Mukherjee. Such a pleasure to have you visit here in Bangalore."

Hardly giving them a chance to answer, he went on. "And such a long journey, you must be tired. You will please dine with us tonight? You are expected by my wife Partha, who even now is preparing a fine south Indian dinner for you. She is a very good cook and most certainly you will not be disappointed."

The doctor finally needed a breath, giving Gran a chance to talk. "Thank you, Dr. Mukherjee. Years ago Shanti wrote to me about her brother."

"Oh, yes. We have many things to talk about."

Ben could guess who would be doing most of the talking.

"I'm anxious to hear how Shanti is," Gran said.

"Let us speak of that later, my dear. Now I want to show you my clinic of which I am very proud." A small, quick-moving man, his feet racing as fast as his mouth, the doctor led them through glass doors into a long hallway, turning his head to keep his conversation going. "Such an honour to have you visit us. I am your new friend, and my wife will be too. Soon I will introduce you to her and to this fine city of Bangalore, most correctly known as the garden jewel of south India. You must please call me Dr. Vivek. All the nurses do."

He surveyed the room proudly. "Such fine nurses we have here. You will be seeing for yourself. They are dedicated to the care of our patients. Yes, our poor patients who ask only that a gentle hand be placed on their forehead when there is nothing more to be done for them."

What was this? Ben's heart started to pound. Surely this place wasn't full of dying people?

Dr. Vivek had paused, but only briefly. "Come with me, one of you on either side. Here we go."

Ben found himself led into a long room as the doctor, hardly stopping for a breath, greeted the nurse at the wood-panelled reception area. Narrow hospital beds lined each wall with nurses in long white saris bending over the patients. There was a strong antiseptic smell, clean but sharp, in the room.

"You see, we have space for twenty-two dying only. We call this a dying home, but in North America I believe you call it a hospice." Dr. Vivek smiled. "But I always say what does a name matter when you are helping people?"

Ben thought he was going to collapse. The email had said it was a clinic. How did this happen? He was in a room full of dying people! "I didn't realize this was a hospice, Dr. Vivek." Ben could hear the shakiness in his voice.

Dr. Vivek went on, "Indeed, most certainly. Here the poor of our city can die with loving care, rather than on the streets alone and suffering. We help who we can, though our place is small and there are so many needy souls."

Ben could do nothing but follow along behind. Every time the doctor stopped for a word or a touch for one of the patients, Ben tried not to look. But wherever he turned, patients were lying back quietly, most of them with their eyes closed. They were probably already dead, Ben thought with horror.

Dr. Vivek stopped at a screen around a bed at the end of the room. Before he could turn away Ben caught a glimpse of an elderly man breathing noisily, with a nurse sitting beside him. Dr. Vivek told the nurse he would come by later.

Ben hadn't been near a dying person since he'd been taken to say goodbye to his father that last day in the Vancouver hospice. Now he was in another hospice. Horrible thoughts flooded into his head and he couldn't pull his mind curtain down to stop them. He was surrounded with dead people. He hated it. He hated it that people had to die. His head was bursting and he wanted to smash something.

The doctor went toward a wide door, talking all the way. "It is most certainly agreed that there is a need here, since many poor people in India do not have a place where they can die in peaceful dignity. Peace and dignity, that is our goal for the end of life."

He opened the door to a veranda. "Now come into the garden while I tell you of my dream."

Ben pushed past Dr. Vivek and ran down the steps. He'd never have come anywhere near this place if he'd known it was a hospice. He ran into a garden along a path bordered with gigantic orange flowers. Their heavy smell brought back the smell of the flowers in his father's hospice room and made Ben feel sick. He'd been in the room with Lauren, Gran and his mother the afternoon his father died.

"He's gone," Ben heard a nurse say. She'd waited while his mother leaned over to kiss his dead father's lips. Then the nurse had led them into another room with a sofa and chairs. She sat with them while a volunteer had brought tea. It had been good to drink something hot.

The nurse had let his mother cry and Gran had held Lauren on her lap. Later the nurse put her arm around Ben. They'd gone back into the room once more to say goodbye. His father was laid out on the bed with a sheet folded under his chin, a peaceful look on his face, and Ben could see his dad wasn't there anymore.

His mother said afterwards she was grateful they'd been in a hospice rather than a regular hospital ward where nurses would be rushing them to leave. They'd been able to stay as long as they wanted. Ben had taken it all for granted. His own feelings had been so overwhelming it hadn't occurred to him to be grateful.

Gran and Dr. Vivek came over to where Ben was standing. Gran spoke to Ben. "I've explained to the doctor that it is not yet a year since your father died. The memories are strong for me too, Ben."

"I am so sorry," Dr. Vivek said. "But I am happy that you were able to be with your father at the end. One should not die alone."

"It's okay," Ben said, staring at his feet. "I'm over it now."

"One is never 'over' such a loss," Dr. Vivek said, looking kindly at Ben. "One simply accepts that death is a part of life."

Gran was looking around the garden. "I'm impressed with what you are doing here, Dr. Vivek."

"You see we have enough space to expand on the grounds around us." He gestured with both arms. "My dream is to put up an addition to the building we have now so there would be space for thirty more patients."

He sighed. "I am talking to people in the community hoping to raise money. The Bangalore municipal government will match what I am able to raise for a simple inexpensive building. Such is my dream."

Dr. Vivek led Gran to a bench, sat beside her and for the first time, stopped talking. He seemed to have run out of things to say and was quietly looking at the site for the new building.

Ben said, "When we went to Varanasi trying to find the Vishnu guest house run by your parents we saw how many people go to die by the Ganges River. In Delhi we saw people who looked dead lying in the street."

"Oh, yes, it is so. There are many sad cases where the poor are not helped to die with dignity. In India there is a great lack of provision for them. Here we can hope to help only a few, but every soul on this earth matters, does it not?"

He paused for another breath and said, "I am sorry to hear that you searched for the guest house by that name in Varanasi. After our parents died, Shanti and her fine husband did run the guest house, but not with that name. After many years Shanti's husband died and now my dear sister lives with her daughter's family."

"How is Shanti now?" Gran asked.

"I will tell you about Shanti in good time. Let us enjoy this garden and the bright blossoms."

"It's a perfect place for a hospice, Dr. Vivek," Gran said, "but I think now I'd like to go back to our hotel to rest."

"I do understand, my dear. And you will come to my simple home for dinner with us tonight?"

"We'd be honoured. Do you promise to talk to me about Shanti?"

"Of course, I will. At great length. Thank you for your interest in my clinic. And now will you kindly allow me to drive you in my humble but safe little car to your hotel?"

The last thing Ben remembered before he fell asleep was lying on his bed in the hotel room and looking at a hand-printed sign on the wall. The sign said:

THE SIZE OF PERSON'S WORLD IS
THE SIZE OF HIS HEART

He'd have to think about that.

Two hours later, he and Gran had rested, showered and changed their clothes and were waiting at the hotel door for Dr. Vivek, who arrived promptly at eight to drive them to his home.

Dr. Vivek's wife asked that they call her Partha. She was round-faced and as plump as a tomato in her red sari, and she proved to be considerably less talkative than her husband but every bit as excited to meet them.

"Come," she said. "Make yourselves comfortable while I finish the last preparations for the meal we will share."

Dr. Vivek offered them a fruit drink, and Gran started to talk about Shanti. "I fear I was unkind to your sister. I hurt Shanti's feelings when I criticized her for allowing her parents to choose a husband. I have regretted my stupidity all these years."

"Come, eat now. We will talk later," Partha said, leading them to a table laden with delicious-smelling curries. "We are vegetarians, but I very much hope you will enjoy what I have cooked for you in the south Indian style."

Partha served *kurma*, a curry with coconut, tomatoes and vegetables; a delicious dish with roasted eggplant called *baigan achari*; and another with cauliflower, potatoes and onions called *aloo gobi*. Dr. Vivek hurried around the table making sure they had helpings of everything, then sat back down and leaned toward Gran. "I am distressed that you blame yourself, dear Norah. It seems to me the misunderstanding was a clash of two very different cultures."

"Now I'm in India, I'm beginning to understand that," Gran said.

Dr. Vivek, who it seemed would rather talk than eat, went on, "I knew about Shanti's Canadian pen pal, but only vaguely. You see I am five years older than my sister, and I was away at school. I do not remember hearing anything about letters stopping."

Ben let Dr. Vivek serve him second helpings. After the shock of finding himself in a hospice this afternoon, he didn't think he'd ever be hungry again, but this was a feast for a rajah. In Vancouver he'd be able to tell Mum and Lauren all the best vegetarian dishes to order in restaurants. They'd be impressed when he talked about *masala dosas*, *biriyani*, *kurma* curry and *aloo gobi*.

Dr. Vivek resumed. "I feel most certain, I want to assure you, that there is some other reason for the letters stopping.

But I do not know what it is, and I am not certain that Shanti will be able to tell you herself."

Ben wondered what Dr. Vivek meant, but Partha interrupted to offer sweet cakes for dessert.

"My favourites," Gran said.

"I am pleased," Partha said, "and I want to assure you that Shanti is not the kind of person to be angry and stop writing. Our Shanti would never do that."

"Like you, Mrs. Norah, Shanti is a gentle woman." Dr. Vivek turned to Gran. "Now that you have finished your meal, I think it is time I told you about her."

He paused for a long time. "I'm not certain how to start . . ." He looked directly at Gran. "You see, all of us get older. Death reaches her fingers out to us more closely every year."

What was this about death reaching out fingers? Ben almost stopped breathing. Shanti was dying. He knew it. He couldn't look at Gran.

Dr. Vivek continued. "Yes, it happens to us all. And for our dear Shanti, it has meant that her memory is the first to be taken away."

Shanti wasn't dying then. She just didn't know who she was.

Gran was wringing her hands in her lap. "Oh, dear. You mean she might not remember me?"

"I cannot say, my dear Norah. Her memory comes and goes. I do not use the word dementia, but I worry that one day, I will."

"Do you think I should visit her?" Gran asked.

"Yes, I most certainly do," Dr. Vivek said. "But you must be prepared that Shanti may remember nothing about you. Could you bear that?"

Gran paused. "I've thought about Shanti for so many years, wondering what was happening in her life and what she looks like. I think if I could just see her, and if she would allow me to hold her hand, it would be worth the trip." Gran lifted her chin. "I'd like to go."

"Well done. You are on the way there now that you are in Bangalore," Dr. Vivek added. "Now you must travel to Delhi by air, then by train to Rishikesh, at the foot of the Himalayan mountains."

"We only have four days left in India," Gran said.

Partha moved her chair closer and put her hand on Gran's shoulder. "You have enough time, my dear. Vivek will reserve tickets and you can leave tomorrow morning. You will be with Shanti by late afternoon."

But will Shanti be with us? Ben still couldn't look at his grandmother. It would be sad for her to discover that Shanti had no idea who she was.

Dr. Vivek started to talk about the planned expansion at his hospice, when Gran sat forward in her chair and spoke. "You know, all over India I've been troubled about beggars. I feel if we give money to them we just encourage them to put their children out to beg. But I want to help the poor in India, and now I can see that your addition would be the perfect way for me to do it. It would be an honour for me to make a donation to your new building."

"Oh, my dear friend," said Dr. Vivek, clearly so overcome he had no more words.

Ben could see that Gran's eyes had a look in them he hadn't seen since his father had died. "I would like to make a donation of three thousand dollars."

"Indeed you are most generous," Partha said.

Dr. Vivek said, "Perhaps we could name the new addition after your son? After Ben's father."

"You mean the Tom Leeson Building?" Ben asked. He had never imagined a building named after his father.

"We are agreed?" asked Dr. Vivek, smiling widely.

"That would be wonderful. Absolutely wonderful," Gran said, beaming back.

"Excellent," Ben said. A place to help other people. It might be a kind of reincarnation for his father. Not the kind of reincarnation Rani talked about where a person came back to live another life, but a way of helping other people after you died. A way you could live on. It made sense. If his father had to die, at least something good would come of it.

Ben watched as Gran wrote a cheque and handed it to Dr. Vivek. She was donating a lot of money, and when the Bangalore government matched it, there would probably be enough for a start on the new building. The Tom Leeson Building.

"My most sincere thanks, dear lady," Dr. Vivek said. He took off his wire-rimmed glasses and wiped them.

"It's my pleasure," Gran said.

In their hotel room, Ben sat down on the bed across from Gran. "I thought your idea for that donation to Dr. Vivek's hospice was awesome. Do you have enough money to do that?"

"I can't think of anything I'd rather give my money to," Gran said, as she crawled into her bed. "It feels better than giving bits of money here and there to beggars. When you told me you'd given your pocket knife to that boy, it made me realize that there are other ways to help. The hospice will make a difference to people, and besides it means there will be a memorial to your father in India, in a country I've cared about for so long."

Ben bent over and gave his grandmother a hug. She hugged him back, and he was reminded how much he used to love her hugs when he was little.

Lying in the narrow bed across the room from his grandmother, Ben said, "It's been like a scavenger hunt, Gran, hasn't it? One thing leads to another and another, and now we're almost at the end of the search."

"It has been like a scavenger hunt, but who knows what kind of a welcome we'll have in Rishikesh."

Ben reached for the top sheet on his bed. His biggest worry now was that Gran might have her heart broken if Shanti didn't recognize her. He had to be prepared for that. He could see himself standing on the streets of Rishikesh holding up his weeping grandmother.

Day Fourteen

"YOU HAVE ARRIVED, madam, sir," said their tonga driver.

Ben read the sign over the Rishikesh hotel: JOURNEY'S END.

From the veranda of their room on the second floor Ben had his first sight of the snow-tipped peaks of the Himalayas. He took a deep breath of the clear air, then turned to the room and tossed his pack on a bed. "Okay, let's go!"

"I'm not ready," Gran sat on a chair by the window, twisting her hands in her lap. "It's almost five o'clock. I'm tired, and I think we should find Shanti tomorrow."

"Gran!" Ben said, whirling around on her. "We've come such a long way already. We've crossed India twice. We've spent hours in planes, cars, trains and buses. How could you think of quitting when we're so close?"

"I'm tired." She slumped in the chair.

"You're stalling. You can't back down now that we're practically on Shanti's doorstep!"

"Maybe we should have something to eat first, Ben," Gran said.

"No. We had lunch on the train. Get with the program." He grabbed his grandmother's arm and steered her to the door. The desk clerk said it was a short walk to Shanti's address on Lapar Road.

The neighbourhood streets were wide and shady, but Gran was moving slower and slower. Ben kept his arm through hers, feeling as though he was dragging her onto Lapar Road. Half a block along, he found a yellow house with vines growing around the door. Number 62 was plainly visible.

He led his grandmother through the gate and up the path. Gran stopped. "The curtains are pulled. You see. No one's home."

"Come on, Gran." Ben tightened his hold on her arm.

"Now that we're so close, I'm afraid. I'm afraid she won't have any idea who I am."

"There's one way to find out. Stand beside me, Gran. Here goes," said Ben. He stepped up to the door and lifted the knocker.

"Wait a minute. What should I say?" Gran whispered, running her hand over her hair.

"I'll speak for you, Gran," Ben said. He dropped the knocker.

The door was opened by a small woman tidily wrapped in a bright blue sari. Her face was lined, and her hair, much greyer than Gran's, was held in a neat twist at the back of her head. The most startling thing about the woman was her eyes, which were filled with light. She said in English, "May I help you?"

Ben cleared his throat. "My grandmother and I have come from Canada and we are looking for Shanti Mukherjee. My grandmother . . ."

The woman looked at them blankly. Ben's heart stopped.

Then the woman's eyes widened as she stared at Gran. "No! Could it be . . . ? Is it you, Norah?" Shanti raised both hands and pressed them to her cheeks.

Gran made a small strangling sound and reached out her arms. "Beloved friend, we meet at last."

Shanti stepped forward, and for what seemed a long time, the two women held onto each other, not speaking, only pulling back for a moment to look into each other's faces and then reaching to hug again.

Ben stood awkwardly on the veranda, his hands shoved deep in his pockets, as his grandmother and Shanti laughed and cried at the same time. He stared at the houses across the street, and when he turned back, Gran was wiping her cheeks. Why did old people cry when they were supposed to be happy?

"Dear Shanti! I can't believe you knew it was me!"

"I know I was a bit slow, dear Norah, but so many years have gone by."

"Fifty years! And it's Ben who found you." Gran turned to Ben, who was shuffling his feet. "Come and meet my Shanti, Ben." Gran was talking quickly now. "Shanti, this is Ben, my grandson and travelling companion."

The small, dark woman turned to Ben and took his hand in both of hers. "Thank you, Ben, for bringing your grand-mother to me."

"You're welcome," Ben said. "I was just lucky." He felt kind of choked up himself. It had taken only a minute for Shanti to recognize Gran. Maybe her brother had been wrong.

"Come in, come in." Shanti motioned them inside the house, leading them through the hallway into a sitting room.

"My daughter and her husband are at work in their sari shop now." Shanti motioned to the sofa. "You must please sit down."

Gran sat on the sofa and Ben took a chair beside the win-dow. Shanti went back and forth between them, patting Ben on the shoulder, then turning to touch Gran, sitting down beside her and getting up again. "I am far too excited to sit. Wait, I have something to show you." She went to the desk and searched through one drawer after another. "I know it's here somewhere. I'm not so good at remembering these days." She pulled out every drawer again and then stood in the middle of the room frowning.

Ben felt sorry for her. She looked so puzzled that she couldn't find what she was looking for, and he didn't know how to help her.

"Oh, I remember now," Shanti said, going over to a small

framed picture on the mantel. "I always keep the photograph up here." She smiled, looking so relieved as she handed Gran a black-and-white photograph in a silver frame.

"You've kept it!" Gran said. Ben leaned over and saw his grandmother as a pretty girl, with her same high forehead and wide smile. Then Gran reached into her backpack and brought out the photograph she'd carried from Vancouver. Ben's eyes went from one to the other. Trying to imagine them as teenagers was as impossible as imagining himself as a sixty-year-old man.

Gran was talking. "I remember when we exchanged these pictures with our letters. We were thirteen, Ben's age. Do you remember I wrote and said I'd come to India one day?"

Shanti put her hand on her heart. "I remember every-thing you wrote, dearest friend. You see my memory for the past remains strong, but these days I sometimes can't recall what I did yesterday. My family worries about me, but I'm not unhappy, especially when the memory of our special friendship is so alive in my heart. And now, at last you are here. Oh, I forget my manners." She jumped up. "Please, I must make you tea."

Ben watched the two women standing side by side in the kitchen, their heads bent together beside the stove where the kettle boiled, Shanti so small and neat in her blue sari, Gran in her long brown skirt. They talked, stopping only to shake their heads or laugh softly.

It felt good to see them together at last. Gran looked so happy and relaxed. And he was proud of himself. Gran was right. He was the one who had found Shanti. With a little help from Dr. Dhaliwal and the internet, Rani and maybe Ganesh, too.

Shanti brought mango juice for Ben and put a plate of sesame honey cakes down beside him. Ben ate the delicious honey cakes while the two grandmothers carried on talking as though he wasn't in the room.

Gran took a deep breath and seemed to have made a decision. "Shanti, I have to talk about something." She moved closer. "It means the world to me that you remember me. I've been afraid you might turn me away. I thought you'd be angry because I questioned your decision to let your parents choose your husband."

Shanti's eyes opened wide. "I was never angry at you, my dear Norah. But I did feel perhaps you might have been angry with me."

"Why would I be angry with you?"

"Because you'd see me as weak for allowing my husband to be chosen for me."

"I questioned it, my dear, but I was never angry."

"Then why didn't you write again?" asked Shanti.

Gran exclaimed, "I did. I *did* write. But there was no answer from you."

"But I answered every letter you wrote."

"What happened to them, I wonder?" Gran said.

Ben wondered why Gran and Shanti hadn't telephoned each other, but in those days phoning would have been expensive and probably most people in India didn't even own phones. Ben thought maybe he should try to help them figure it out. "It's strange," he said. "Did either of you move?"

"I did," Shanti said. "I moved to Delhi when I married. Shortly after that, my parents moved from Agra to manage the hotel in Varanasi so my old address would have changed."

"We know about those moves. My grandmother and I have been following that trail, but isn't there a system for forwarding mail in India?" Ben asked.

Shanti nodded. "Now, yes, but perhaps not in those days. I'm sure I sent you my new address, Norah. I wonder why my letters didn't come to you?"

"Did *you* move anywhere, Gran?" Ben asked.

"Actually I did. It was right around that time that I began my travels and went to live in England for eighteen months," Gran said, "but my parents would have sent on any letters from Shanti." She thought for a minute. "You know, there was a long postal strike when I first went overseas. I remember I was upset when I didn't hear from my parents for more than a month."

Ben had an idea. "My guess is that Shanti's letters could have been lost in the postal strike."

"That might be it," Gran said. "And then, I stopped writing because I was certain you never wanted to hear from me again."

"I stopped writing for the same reason," Shanti said, nodding her head. "I thought you saw me as a silly Indian woman with no mind of my own."

Shanti and Gran were so absorbed in each other they'd

forgotten him. He sat there like an invisible man. Ben took the last sesame honey cake and glanced around the room. There were pictures along the top of the mantle and a long dining room table in the next room.

Gran was saying, "How foolish and strong-headed we both were." She put her hand over Shanti's. "Were you happy in your marriage?"

That was his grandmother. Always wanting to talk about people's feelings. How much longer would this kind of talk go on?

Shanti smiled. "It was a happy marriage. My parents chose wisely for me. My husband was a good man." She wrinkled her brow as she tried to concentrate. "Now I live here with my daughter's family. My oldest grandson is studying computers in the south, and the youngest is still at school. Rajiv will be home soon."

"I chose my own husband," Gran said, "and we were happy. But I've been widowed for ten years now. Ben's father was my only child. He died not quite a year ago."

"He would have been young," said Shanti. "My poor Norah. So hard to lose your son." She turned to Ben. "I am so sorry, Ben, that you are without your father now."

The one thing Ben didn't like was sympathy. He needed some fresh air. He leapt to his feet. "Okay if I go outside and have a look around?"

"Of course, Ben," said Shanti. "Go out the back door and see what you can find."

The garden was full of plants with spiky flowers and a tall

fig tree, but what caught Ben's attention was a green parrot perched in a cage hanging from the tree. The parrot hopped back and forth on a bar, cocking his eye to look at Ben and squawking loudly. There was a box of peanuts beside the cage and Ben began tossing them to the parrot when he heard a voice behind him. "Don't feed Mikul too many or he'll get sick. Being a Canadian you've probably never been around a sick parrot, but it is not a pretty sight."

The speaker was a boy about his age, though smaller. He had dark hair that stood more or less straight up and he was grinning. "I'm Rajiv. I came in through the front and met your grandmother. Welcome to India, Ben."

"Thanks. Our grandmothers used to be pen pals," Ben said.

"They're in the house talking like two crazy parrots!"

"It was too much for me," Ben said.

"I think we should get out of here. Like a ride on my scooter?" Rajiv asked.

"I'm there," Ben said.

The boys rushed into the house to grab helmets.

Ben didn't want to admit he'd never ridden a scooter before. At the side of the house he got on behind Rajiv, who kick-started the engine and headed onto the road with Ben holding on tightly to his jacket. The wind rushed past Rajiv and onto Ben's face as they steered around rickshaws, buses and trucks to the edge of town. Rajiv slowed the scooter at a wooden gate in front of a park. "That's our famous elephant reserve."

"I seem to have been following elephants all over India. Think I could see these?" Ben asked.

"No problem. I'll take you tomorrow."

Ben laughed. "You say 'no problem' up here too!"

"That's just the way life is in India. No problem!" Rajiv called, revving up the engine again. They circled back through town and crossed onto Lapar Road.

They arrived just as Shanti's daughter and her husband came home from the shop. Savita was a smaller version of her mother, with dark hair that came down to the middle of her back. Uday, her husband, with hair that stood up like Rajiv's, shook hands to welcome Ben and Norah.

Later, they all sat down in the dining room for a celebration meal cooked by Savita. Toasts were made to the reunion of the grandmothers, to the grandchildren, to India and to Canada. Most of the time, Shanti seemed to be involved, but Ben noticed that often she'd peer around the table in a bewildered way as the conversation went on without her.

Gran tapped Shanti's shoulder. "Do you remember telling me that your brother talked all the time? He still talks a lot, doesn't he?"

Shanti's face brightened. "Vivek is such a sweet man, but he can be a chatterbox. He also worries about me too much. I know my memory isn't as good as it used to be, but my daughter's family takes care of me." Shanti smiled around the table.

Gran said, "You certainly remembered *me*! I'm just sorry

we only have a few more days before we fly back to Vancouver."

Shanti answered. "I would never forget you, dear Norah, but it makes me sad that we have only a short time together."

Gran nodded. "It took us two days to try to find your parents' address at the registry office, then we travelled to Agra and Varanasi and after that I gave up and we went to stay at the beach in Mahabalipuram. Then I got sick."

Ben told everyone how Gran had to be taken to the hospital. Shanti was horrified to think that Gran had been so ill.

"But if Gran hadn't got sick," Ben said, "we never would have met the doctor who told us about your brother."

"You're right, Ben," Rajiv said.

"I was so impressed, Shanti, with what your brother is doing with the hospice," Gran said. She told the family that Ben's father had died in a hospice and how she'd decided to contribute toward the new wing of Dr. Vivek's hospice.

Shanti and Gran hugged and cried all over again.

Rajiv tapped Ben on the shoulder. "Come and see my computer." The expression on Ben's face when he got to Rajiv's room and saw all the latest computer technology made Rajiv laugh. "A lot of people around the world don't realize when they contact their computer servers with a problem, they're usually talking to technicians here in India."

Rajiv's room, with its posters of rock stars, piles of messy clothes and an unmade bed, looked remarkably like Ben's own room.

Rajiv leaned against the wall. "It's great that you came all the way over here with your grandmother."

"It's been quite a trip. Not always great travelling with an older person. We've had our moments."

"I can believe it," Rajiv said, "though your grandmother seems sharp. Sometimes now when my grandmother is confused and forgets things, it's hard to know how to handle it. My mother says not to judge, just keep on loving her."

At least Gran didn't get confused. And people always seemed to like her. Maybe it was easier to like someone if they weren't related to you. Maybe he should stop judging everything she did.

When they came downstairs there was talk about the next day. Shanti's daughter and husband had to work, so Gran and Shanti would have lots of time together.

"Ben and I will be spending all day at the elephant reserve," Rajiv added.

"I'm there," Ben said.

Back at the hotel, Gran went up to bed and Ben found a computer in the hotel lobby.

Dear Mum and Lauren

You won't believe it but we found Shanti today. Her memory isn't very good but, almost right away, she knew who Gran was. C U in 3 days, counting the time change.

Ben

Ben sat at the computer thinking about his conversation with Rajiv about grandmothers. When he was little, he and Gran would say "Love you" to each other every time they said goodbye. Somehow, as he grew up, he'd stopped answering her, and now he couldn't remember the last time they'd said it.

Before he went to bed, he had a special email to send.

Dear Rani

We've found Shanti here in Rishikesh. You can imagine the reunion – tears everywhere. Gran has decided to sponsor a new wing of a hospice run by Shanti's brother in Bangalore so I'll be going to see it when I come back to India. Think I'll come to Mahabalipuram first if that's all right with you!? Say hi to your mother and Prem. Tell him No Problem about anything! Next time you hear from me I'll be at my own computer in Vancouver. You'd better answer my emails.

Namaste Ben

Then Ben deleted his request on the school site. Good old Ganesh had helped him, but not in the way he'd expected.

Days Fifteen & Sixteen

"YOU SURE YOUR brother won't mind?"

"I'm sure. He used to lend me his scooter before I got my own. Just remember to keep your left foot on the ground when you start the engine."

Ben stepped down hard on the kick starter. The engine sputtered. Rajiv reached over and turned the throttle in the handle. Ben stepped harder and the engine sputtered briefly again, then stopped. He tried twice more until Rajiv told him he'd flooded the carburetor and had to wait.

Ben hoped his grandmother couldn't hear them, but the noise of the engine brought Gran and Shanti to the side of the house.

"Do you know how to ride one of those bikes, Ben?" Gran asked.

"Yep, and Rajiv is helping me," Ben answered.

"Don't you need a licence?"

"Not for scooters," Rajiv said.

"Be careful." Ben couldn't believe his ears when that was all his grandmother said.

Rajiv adjusted the choke and Ben tried again. This time the engine caught and vibrated reassuringly. He let out the clutch and his bike moved ahead. Ben would have liked to wave goodbye but didn't dare lift his hand off the handlebars.

There wasn't much traffic on the road, and after a few wobbles, Ben got the hang of it. He kept his eye on Rajiv as he followed behind, on guard for stray dogs, pot holes and Rajiv's brake light. After they reached the edge of town, Rajiv turned into the parking lot of the elephant reserve and showed Ben where to park the scooter.

"That was a sweet ride!" Ben exclaimed, taking off his helmet.

"You were brilliant for your first time," Rajiv said, leading Ben to the entrance. Inside, a small barefoot man in a white dhoti greeted them. In good English he introduced himself as Gopal, their guide for the day. "I am a *mahout*, an elephant keeper, and have worked with elephants all my life." As they walked along a path, Gopal rolled up his sleeve to reveal a ragged scar. "I carry this as a reminder of the time I was charged by a wild boar some years ago in the south."

Gopal looked at the boys' faces and laughed. "No need to worry. Here we have only birds, monkeys and deer that live peacefully with the magnificent animals you have come to visit."

Gopal led them across a bridge onto a raised wooden walkway under a canopy of trees that were filled with the noisy chatter of a flock of parrots. Below them, Ben spotted two grazing deer. Gopal nodded. "You have good eyes for a visitor."

They came to a clearing, where a platform overlooked a large pool. Six adult elephants with two of their young stood in the mud, dipping their trunks into the water and curling them to their mouths to drink. One of the larger elephants in deeper water tossed sprays of water from its trunk onto its back. The two little ones played around the legs of the adults.

Ben remembered the poor chained elephant at Kali's temple. What a different life that sad creature led.

Gopal signalled the boys to follow him down the steps. "We will approach the herd slowly. Since we are not busy today, you may help wash the babies."

The elephants shifted their huge heads to watch the visitors. Their ears flapped and their enormous feet squished the mud. Low grunts and snorts sounded as if they were having a conversation. Ben sniffed the air: the strong smell of elephants.

Gopal went to a shed and took out hand brushes and

pails. At the sound of the shed door opening, the little elephants came running up, laying their small trunks along Gopal's arm and sniffing at Ben and Rajiv. The smell of humans, Ben thought.

The young elephants were the same height as the boys. Ben noticed their spiky eyelashes and touched the trunk of the smallest elephant. It was double the size of his own arm, and it felt soft and firm at the same time. The elephant curled its trunk around Ben's arm and nuzzled the tip into his neck. The wet lips sucked at Ben's skin.

"Rajiv has the male. He's five months and his name is Pad," Gopal said. "And Ben, your little one is a female, just four months. We call her Pot. They are cousins, and the large females are their mothers, aunts and grown sisters."

"You mean they're all related?" Ben asked.

"Yes," Gopal said. "We don't keep adult males here. Pad will be moved away when he is three or four years old. Grown males can be aggressive, so we arrange visits once a year. You can guess why," Gopal giggled behind his hand. Rajiv cast an amused glance at Ben.

Gopal handed the boys two lengths of green sugar cane. "A treat for the little ones today."

Pot came rushing over on her short legs and grabbed the cane from Ben with her trunk and popped it into her mouth. The snap and crunch her of chewing reminded him of his sister eating popcorn in front of the television.

"Time for a bath," Gopal said. The boys sloshed pails

of water over the animals, who shivered in delight. They scrubbed them from their broad backs down to their feet, going back over their domed heads and around the small trunks.

"They love this!" Ben said. He asked Gopal to get his camera out of his pack to take pictures of the two of them washing the elephants.

"Don't forget to clean their ears," Gopal said. "The little ones seem to get lots of mud in there." Every time Ben lifted his arm to scrub Pot's ear, she pushed her cold trunk into his armpit, drenching him before he could shove her away. Afterwards, the small elephants ran around the compound, flapping their ears to dry themselves.

"Now, young men, your reward for the hard work is an elephant ride," Gopal said.

"Brilliant!" Ben exclaimed. At last, his chance to ride an elephant.

"We'll go together on Purna, Pad's mother. She's forty-eight years old and as easygoing as they come." Gopal took his metal-tipped stick and gently tapped Purna's shoulder to separate her from the others. Ben was relieved that he didn't prod with the stick, just used it to guide her.

Purna lumbered toward them and lowered her trunk to the ground. Gopal hopped up on it and in a flash was swung onto the top of the elephant's head. He pointed to the platform. "You boys get on that way."

Ben asked, "Could I get up on Purna's trunk, please?"

Gopal nodded, signalling the elephant to lower her trunk; Ben threw his leg over and climbed on.

Gopal called, "Don't stand like I did. Sit and lean forward. Hold on tight."

The next thing Ben knew he was high in the air atop the huge animal's back. What a ride! "Want to come up this way, Rajiv?"

"I'm there!" Rajiv said, climbing onto Purna's trunk. When both boys were seated behind Gopal, Purna began her long lumbering steps along the path. Ben thought he'd never be able to explain what sitting on a moving elephant was like. Feeling very unstable and high up, you were lurched forward and swayed from side to side at the same time. It was like a crazy ride at the PNE. Rajiv kept a firm hold on Ben's waist and he tightened his own arms around Gopal.

Just as Ben got used to Purna's lurching and swaying, the path into the jungle led through trees with long branches extending across the trail. They had to duck fast to avoid getting knocked on the head. They were so high in the air that, when Gopal pointed to a group of monkeys playing in the trees, the noisy monkeys were at eye level.

"These are the black-faced langur monkeys," Gopal explained. The monkeys had halos of white hair around their dark faces; their grimaces and smacking sounds were so funny the boys had to laugh. Startled, the monkeys cast their sharp eyes at the intruders and swung away through the trees, tails-over-arms in a leaf-shattering group.

Jungle smells drifted up to Ben, smells of damp foliage and rich soil and, above all, the smell of an elephant under you. Purna's rough skin felt warm against his legs. He thought of the carving inside the beach cave; the boy's excited face as he rode the elephant. He was sure his own face had the same look.

Ben felt he had a grin on his face all the way back to Shanti's house on the scooter. They parked the bikes and rushed into the house, where Gran and Shanti were still talking.

"We washed the little elephants and we rode through the jungle on their mother. It was excellent," Ben told Gran. "I've got great pictures of us washing Pot and Pad for my school report."

Rajiv grabbed some of Shanti's coconut cookies for himself and Ben and called, "We're going to change our wet clothes. I'm taking Ben to do some shopping in town. Meet you at the sari shop at five o'clock."

In a shop down a side street, Ben spent the rest of the money Uncle Bob had given him. For Lauren, he found an ankle bracelet with silver bells, just like the one Rani wore. He bought a rose-coloured shawl for his mother, and for himself, a brass board game played with tigers and goats. The winner of the game held the tiger that captured all the goats. One other present was tucked in his pack.

In the sari shop, Rajiv's mother was showing Gran the bolts of silk that lined the walls. Arranged by colours, the rolls transformed the shop walls into a silky rainbow.

Shanti was talking to Gran. "I'd like to give you a gift of a sari, my dear. Would you accept that?"

"I've wanted a sari ever since we arrived," Gran said. "They are so graceful on Indian women, but I wonder, is it proper for a westerner to wear your traditional dress?"

"Of course, especially when it is a gift," Shanti smiled. "Now you must choose a colour."

Gran studied one wall and then another, stopping to run her fingers over a soft yellow or rich violet silk. Savita pulled out the bolts, flipping out a length of fabric and gathering it over her arm to show how the silk glowed. "When you have chosen," she said, "our tailor will make up a matching blouse for you. He will make it by this evening."

Shanti strolled over to Ben and Rajiv, standing near the door. She peered closely at Ben. "Who do we have here?"

Rajiv grabbed his grandmother's arm and whispered, "It's Ben."

Shanti seemed confused.

"You know, Norah's grandson from Canada," Rajiv said.

Suddenly Shanti smiled. "Oh, yes, of course. Ben. Aren't I silly!" She smiled a little uncertainly and wandered back to the others.

"Sorry, Ben. That sometimes happens, even with me," Rajiv said.

"No problem," Ben said. He decided there was no need to upset Gran by telling her.

Gran had chosen a pale green sari with a gold border, and

she went with Shanti into the dressing room to learn how to drape the long fabric into a skirt and then into a long shawl over her shoulder. When she came out, Gran's face glowed, and she twirled in circles, getting herself so dizzy she nearly fell over. For once, Ben didn't feel embarrassed.

Walking back, Ben came across a statue of Ganesh on a street corner. "Mind if we stop for a minute?" he asked Rajiv.

Ganesh sat on a platform, fat-bellied and smiling, his trunk curling down over his crossed legs. A bowl of candies sat by his bare feet. As Ben looked into the statue's eyes, he once again had a strong feeling that Ganesh was looking back at him. Then, standing on the Rishikesh street, with the noise and bustle of the people and the traffic around him, Ben said, "Thanks, Ganesh."

"What did you say?" Rajiv said.

"Nothing. It's just that Ganesh is special to me."

"You know, I think of him as my friend."

Yes, Ben thought. I do too.

That night the two families had dinner at a restaurant; toasts were made with spicy tea, and plans were discussed for their last day in Rishikesh. The following day Ben and Gran would take the train to catch their plane in Delhi.

It was decided that they would all drive up the mountain to see the source of the Ganges River. Savita and Uday would take the day off work, and they'd leave early in the morning.

On the way back to their hotel, the almost full moon sent a track of luminescence over the town. Lights were strung in trees along the temple paths, bells rang out in the night air and the smell of smoke from cooking fires came from all directions. Somewhere, not far away, worshippers were chanting.

"Are you happy to be with Shanti at last, Gran?" Ben asked.

"I am very happy," was the answer from his sleepy grandmother.

"Bring your jackets. It's cold in the mountains," Shanti cautioned as the six of them piled into Uday's small car the next morning. The road turned and twisted as it clung to the sides of ascending foothills. On one side there was a dense forest; on the other, a sheer drop. After a long drive, they parked the car and followed a narrow trail lined with moss and overhung with tall pines. The air was sparkling cold and Ben was glad he'd packed his jacket, even though this was the first time he'd worn it in India. The air was filled with Rajiv's whistling.

Ben turned to see why Rajiv was whistling so much and saw Rajiv's mouth closed in a smile.

"How did you do that?" Ben asked.

"It's not me." Rajiv said with a wide grin. "That's the whistling thrush. I was hoping there'd be one today!"

"You're kidding me."

"See, in the trees there, that bright blue bird?"

Just as Ben caught a flash of colour, the bird flew off, leaving the ring of its almost human whistle lingering along the swooping branches of the pines.

High above him the white peaks of the Himalayas pushed against the sky. A giant slab of an age-old glacier sat like frosting along the nearest high ridge. The air was so clear Ben felt he could reach to the top of the highest mountain range in the world.

Ahead of them on the trail, Shanti, Gran and Savita in their saris looked like bright birds themselves. They had stopped to see the wild orchids Shanti found growing on the forest floor.

The trail led steeply down to a narrow path along the ravine. The boys ran ahead, flinging their arms wide on either side, pretending to fly. Ben felt he *could* almost fly to Mount Everest. From the top of the world he'd be able to look out over India, Nepal and Tibet, maybe even China.

"We're here," Rajiv called as he and Ben reached a viewing stand above the ravine. Down below, huge boulders had tumbled down the mountain. Between them, foaming and sparkling, flowed the beginnings of the Ganges River.

"The source," Gran said, out of breath as she reached the viewing deck.

"This is where our beloved Ganga begins its journey across India," Uday explained.

"Remember the carvings we saw at Mahabalipuram, Ben?" Gran said.

"Yes, the gods and animals and humans coming out of the river," Ben said. He remembered Rani showing him the carving of Ganesh.

Gran smiled at Shanti. "Yes, and it feels as if you and I have returned to the source of our friendship."

Shanti looked at the two boys who were clambering over the trail above the viewing spot. "Yes, my dear, and now we have the great pleasure of watching as our grandchildren become friends." Gran wrapped her arm around Shanti's narrow shoulders.

Ben took photographs of the water coming out of the rocks and one of Rajiv poking his head out behind a rock, grinning, his hair standing straight up. He took another picture of Shanti with Gran's arm around her shoulders.

Savita and Uday turned to go back down the trail, and Rajiv took his grandmother's arm to walk with her. Ben and Gran stayed a few moments, not speaking as they looked down on the newborn river. This river would gain in size and speed for its long journey across the wide Indian subcontinent. It would cross the central plain, nourishing rice paddies and fields of vegetables to feed a billion people. It would flow through Varanasi where floating marigolds and candles drifted beside the ashes of the dead. The river would continue across to the Bay of Bengal, where Ben had swum in the warm water with a beautiful girl named Rani.

Ben thought about everything he'd seen in India. He thought about the people they'd met: their first taxi drivers, serious Madhu and toothless Padam; little Harish and his mother that first day in the registry office; Anoop, their boatman in Varanasi; Dr. Vivek and his wife in Bangalore;

and most of all Ben thought about Rani and Prem and their mother — especially Rani.

Here at the source of this river, they'd found Shanti and their journey had ended. Ben looked at his grandmother. She had brought him to India. No one else he knew had a grandmother like her. She turned to look at him and he smiled.

Gran smiled back. "Love you, Ben."

"Love you."

"Time for us to go home," Gran said.

Day Seventeen

SHANTI AND RAJIV HAD insisted on travelling with them on the early morning train. Just before they arrived in Delhi they shared the box lunch Shanti and her daughter had packed.

At the Delhi railway station, they squeezed into a taxi to the airport. It was strange to be in Delhi's hectic traffic after their quiet time in Rishikesh. At the airport, Ben walked through the crowd beside the others, then paused as he heard once again the call of the muezzin. He remembered puzzling about the strange sound his first morning in India. He'd learned a lot about India since that day.

As he hurried to catch up with the others who were

nearing the entrance to the terminal, a hand gripped his shoulder. "Ben sahib!"

Ben turned quickly and was astounded to see Padam with Madhu's shiny bald head close behind.

"Ben sahib! Norah memsahib! Good golly! What amazing luck we are having here!" Padam said in his high voice, his wide grin showing his pink gums.

"I don't believe it!" Gran said.

"Great to see you!" Ben said, putting out his hand.

"All the days we have been searching for you," Madhu said, shaking hands vigorously. "Your journey, has it been successful?"

"Oh, yes," Gran said. "We've found Shanti! We found her in Rishikesh." She introduced Shanti and Rajiv.

They crowded together, all talking at once, Padam jumping up and down with excitement. Shanti and Rajiv had heard about the taxi drivers from Delhi and were pleased to meet them.

"Tell us your news. How has it been in Delhi?" Gran asked.

"We are well," said Madhu, "and our taxi business is as good as ever."

"But it is most sad-sad as we are having no more charming Canadian passengers, only Americans and Germans!" Padam said. "Good golly! Now good fortune is ours and we are meeting once again." He looked as though he'd burst.

"Of course we have been thinking and talking of you many times. You are in our hearts forever," Madhu said.

"And you in ours. Your country too," Gran answered.

It was time to check in for the flight, and after group photographs it was a solemn moment as they said goodbye with final *namastes* to the two drivers who had become their friends. Then Shanti and Gran put their arms around each other for a long farewell. Ben checked that he had Rajiv's email address and promised to send photographs.

Ben took his grandmother's hand and led her to the departure gate, where they turned to wave goodbye. Their Indian friends were waving, but to Ben they already seemed far away.

On board the plane, Ben stretched out in the seat by the window. He looked at his grandmother, dressed in her green and gold sari, staring out the window, not even bothering to wipe the tears that rolled down her cheeks.

"You'll never lose touch with Shanti again, Gran," he said.

"I know that, Ben. These are tears of happiness now." She smiled, and for the first time Ben realized she had his father's smile. Why had he never noticed that?

As the plane lifted into the air, Ben thought of Lauren. She had that same smile too. Maybe that was another way a person's spirit could live on. His dad would live on in the smiles and the memories of the people who'd loved him. It would be good to see Lauren again and find out how her hockey team was doing.

As the plane gained altitude, Ben looked down at the

thousands of houses and streets, the maze of millions of people that had surprised him when he'd arrived in India. He knew some of those people now. Knew them and cared about them, especially about a girl who built sandcastles like the Taj Mahal.

Ben settled in his seat. "Mission accomplished, Gran."

"Indeed, and you've been the best of travelling companions, Ben," Gran said. She handed Ben a small, heavy parcel. Ben unwrapped a brass statue of a seated god, the perfect size to fit his hand. It was Ganesh with the same smile, the same pudgy belly and the same curved trunk. His own elephant boy to take home.

"This is amazing and I know right where it's going. On the top of my computer!"

"Don't tell me getting back to that computer is all you can think about, Ben!" Gran said, laughing.

"Don't worry. I won't have time to play computer games. I've got my digital pictures to organize and a report to write for school, and I will be using it to email Rani and Rajiv."

Ben turned the statue over. Such a funny god with his large elephant head and sturdy boy's legs. "You know, kids in India believe that Ganesh helps overcome obstacles."

"Our trip had more than a few of those," Gran said.

Ben grinned at his grandmother. "It was epic!" He reached in his pocket for a small package and handed it to Gran. "Thanks for taking me with you."

Gran was speechless as she held the delicate silver elephant up by the chain.

"You could say we were with elephants all the way, couldn't you?" Ben said.

Gran put the chain around her neck. "Thank you, Ben. I love this."

The flight attendants brought their last Indian meal, and the two travellers settled back in their seats.

"Remember that saying in our guidebook?" Gran said. "Something like, a traveller goes to India seeking adventure. What he finds is himself."

"I didn't know what it meant. Did you find *yourself*, Gran?"

"I guess in a way I did. When I found Shanti, I found an answer to what had been an empty space in my heart. Shanti told me her name means peace and that's what I've found."

Ben looked out the window. They were above the clouds now. Ahead, on the horizon of an enormous dark sky, he could see only a small rim of red. The sun had set on their last day in India.

Gran turned toward him. "What about you, Ben? Did you find out anything about yourself?"

It was hard to find the words. Ben looked at Ganesh in his hand. "I guess I did. I found out there are some things in life I can't explain."

He paused. "And I learned that I can't be angry about death because it's part of life."

"That's a lot to learn in seventeen days."

"Yep."

ACKNOWLEDGEMENTS

There is a real Shanti in my life. She was my pen pal when I was in grade school, and later we lost touch with each other. I have always longed to find her but had no success in my three visits to India. All I have now is one of her letters and a small black and white photograph, but I also have wonderful memories of India, and a strong connection to my foster son, Natarajan, who lives in Bangalore. In *Follow the Elephant* I had the opportunity to rewrite history and let Ben, the troubled grandson, find Shanti.

I am grateful for the help of the boys: Zac Pollard, Noah Abramson, Mac Macdonald and Sam Fraser, who patiently undertook to teach me about computer language and PlayStations.

I want to thank my smart and supportive community of women friends who stood by me through the years I worked on this book: Shelley Hrdltischka, Roberta Rich, Louise Hager, Barbara Clague, Linda Bailey, Velma Moore, Norma Charles, Merry Wood, Margaret Prang, Margot Young, Shelley Mason, Dianne Tullson, Heather Kelleher, Carol Dale, Susan Moger, Bakhti Bonner, Madeleine Nelson, Anne Fraser, Dianne Woodman and Jeannie Corsi.

Along the way I received valuable help from Lata Sood, Shauna Mansahia, Ameen Merchant, Ellen Clague, Ann-Marie Metten, Ram Crowell, Ken Pederson, Brian Young, Kulwant Ranji and from Terry Jordan and his writing group. I want to thank Paula Jane Remlinger and the board at the Sage Hill Writing Experience for their financial support.

I owe special gratitude to my friend Tom Blom, who is now deceased. With his unique charm and sensitivity, Tom saw me through early drafts of this book.

I was extremely fortunate to have Ronald and Veronica Hatch as my editors. They share my love of India and possess editing skills based, not just on where the commas go, but on a deep understanding of Indian culture.

Many thanks to my steadfast agent Beverley Slopen, who followed this pachyderm along with me.

About the Author

Beryl Young is the author of the best-selling young adult novel *Wishing Star Summer* (Raincoast, 2001) and *Charlie: A Home Child's Life in Canada* (Key Porter, 2009). She is a member of the Federation of BC Writers, the Children's Writers and Illustrators of BC, the Writers' Union of Canada, and the Canadian Society of Authors, Illustrators and Performers. She has a passion for elephants and for India where she has travelled three times in an unsuccessful search for her real life pen pal. She has three children and four grandchildren and lives in Vancouver.